MS. ANGEL'S POET

BY

TCHINDA FABRICE MBUNA

MS. ANGEL'S POET

BY

TCHINDA FABRICE MBUNA

Published by Tchinda Mbuna Books
Published in United States

2023

Copyright © 2023 by Tchinda Fabrice Mbuna

Library of Congress Control Number: 2023906181
ISBN: Softcover   978-1-955963-19-0
        Hardcover   978-1-955963-22-0
        Ebook   978-1-955963-24-4

DEDICATION

To her excellency of my heart,
In my heart's weed, she weeds,
In my heart's weed, she is the wit
Of what my heart delights with.

To her excellency of my heart,
Blessed is the day we did meet.
I can assure you; she isn't a mitt.
In all storms, she can cope or fit.

In all my heart's squares, she fits
The mother queen of love in her outfit.
Always classic, not to be a misfit,
And always on heels, never bare feet.

Her name is Bessi but call her Madam Mbuna.
She's all in one, pretty like a Mbuna.
You can also call her the real Miss Angel,
Everything about her is of a divine angel.
When you give her love,
She multiplies and gives you more.
When you give her peace,
She does increase your peace and grease!

She's my heart's garden flower
Which gladdens my heart forever!
More peace and love that will never
Be drained by chagrin or by any means severed.

Bessi, your love is treasured,
Noble and even lettered.
You made our love a nest, so secretive
Like Blue Jays, you are daring and protective.

You fight with the might of a crowned eagle

Who else deserves such honor or regal?
What is of your equal – raven, cockatoo, or crow?
You're the finest of all, and will always glow!

Also, to them all; my sons and daughters,
Wendy, Katriel, Samuel, Karen, my laughter.
You've made me a happy father.
My heart is delighted to see you grow farther.

I have begun a trip; you must keep the journey,
Life is a journey, not always sweet as honey.
Never a bed of roses will it ever be
As prophesied, though contracted with a rose.

'You will see racism, injustice; don't bother.
Keep moving, keep loving each other.
Be each other's keeper as an honored potter,
Bear each other's burdens and avoid unnecessary pother.'

You are the arrows of my youth or vitality,
Be the light of the world; avoid whimsicality.
Be the salt of the earth, the pride of morality,
Be the glory of the world, the pride of divinity.

Do good all the time; life is full of eventuality,
For God has endowed in you grace of hospitality.
When you age, age with graceful vitality,
But never forget life hereafter or immortality.

Your father, Mbuna!
Your best friend, Mbuna!
A heart beats for you, Mbuna!
Endless love from Mbuna!

To My Beloved Parents

Father: John Claude Mbuna

Mother: Helen Fobah Mbuza.

ACKNOWLEDGMENT

We're all made of clay, with a fragile frame.
It does not matter one's color, race, or name.
Today we might be young; tomorrow, we'll be old.
Life is a rough stage for all; one must be bold.
Today we might be rich, tomorrow as a pauper.
Life does not seem to be fair or always proper.
With age comes maturity, love, and compassion.
When I was a child, I spoke like one with passion.

As a grown-up man, I speak more with tenderness
As a grown-up, I speak more with cleverness.
Life sets before us all a stage for us to act.
Everyone is free to act or choose to react.
One does not need to be a trained actor
Neither does one need to be a trained orator
To play his or her own role on the stage of life.
Be it rich or poor, black, or white, we all strife.

It is a global crisis called the crisis of parenting.
No parent is perfect; all of us as parents are wanting.
Life Is a stage but, at the same time, a school of learning.
We are teachers to ourselves, via our experiences.
We were all born to parents, some with inexperiences.
To Mr. John Claud Mbuna and Ms. Helen F. Mbuza
I am grateful for their sacrifice of love and care.
Life might not have treated you well or seemed fair.

Your past is past, a teacher from whom I have learned
That age does not deter us from erring or being burned
By our mistakes and fallibility as we seek perfection.
I am forever indebted for having a father and mother.
Your failures have taught me to love one another.
I was a broken vessel in the hands of a divine potter
Now, I am striving for betterness and not bitterness.

Old things have passed; all things are now new

I am a new creation, like heaven's fresh dew.
I want to say I love you and will forever will
For the man, I am today, a man of free will.
May you age with grace and see your grandkids
I will teach them the lessons learned from life as a kit.

TABLE OF CONTENTS

SYNOPSIS OF MISS ANGEL

A versified autobiographical depiction of the life of Tchinda Fabrice Mbuna and the writing of *Miss Angel*, *Mrs. Angel*, *Miss Seraphim* book series, this work introduces and navigates us through his personal life from infancy, upbringing, education, and life challenges till the time he begins his creative writing career as a poet and playwright.

FOREWORD

A plethora of present-day writers have so soon forgotten their role as "the gadflies and goads of the society" as opined by Socrates. The only reason why they write is to sell their books as quickly as possible and get rich overnight. Their greatest achievement for writing is to be called 'Bestwellers.' They only write to please their audience. They don't write to be rejected by the majority and be accepted by the minority. If this happens, they would call themselves failures. All they care about is making money with their books. They don't care about the declining moral values in the society. They don't give a damn to it. It is not their business.

Plato contended, "The price good men pay for being indifferent to public affairs is to be ruled by evil men."
In *Ms. Angel's Poet*, Tchinda Fabrice Mbuna identifies himself as a good man, and refuses to be indifferent to public affairs and consequently pay the price of being ruled by evil men. Backed by his divine authority, he rebukes the ongoing evil in America pell-mell. He identifies himself as God's anointed, and refuses to sit and fold his arms like a statue and watch the American society going morally bankrupt and facing perpetual damnation in his on-looking eyes. He must ring the bell of warning in their ears monotonously. Now or never!

Aung Sang Suu Kyi said, "You should never let your fears prevent you from doing what is right." On his part, Immanuel Kant said, "If the truth shall kill them, then, let them die." In this his autobiography, Tchinda Fabrice Mbuna has shunned fear and mustered courage to speak the truth to America in her face cartes sur table. That's not all. He has seized America by the collars of her shirt, summoned her to the conference table of atonement and compelled her to humble herself as seen in the following citation:

America must at all cost address today's atrocity,

14

Not with racial pride or brutish police viscosity,
But with its diplomacy, and even so, generosity.

Ms. Angel's Poet is a vivid recount of the childhood, education, and journey of the author as a young man from his country, Cameroon to America, the challenges of his new environment, and his efforts to face them accordingly. Wholly presented in verse, and deliberately impregnated with a multitude of high-minded themes like nostalgia, religion, education and diplomacy inter alia, the author distinguishes himself as not only a consummate verse raconteur, but also a socio-political, economic, social and literary critic of the caliber of Alexander Pope to be reckoned with.

Nowadays, very few writers invest heavily in content, form and structure, but in this **magnum opus**, Fabrice invests lavishly in the said trio artistic nomenclature. This kind of expensive investment is only given to an erudite. As an emerging African writer too, and a literary mentor with twenty-seven years of severe formation, if I am handed the microphone by an international media journalist to tell the world my impression about Tchinda Fabrice Mbuna, I would simply say that the nation of Cameroon should be proud of not only a son of the soil, but a son of heaven in the Diaspora.

Nkwetatang Sampson Nguekie,
Literary Mentor & Facilitator,
Bamenda, Cameroon.

THE PROLOGUE

My life, my story, much like a fairy tale,
A tale like that of the famous Chaucer,
In Canterbury, where he wrote as a scholar,
I will be truthful; I promise you not to fail
With any detail of my life worth some dollars.
The journey is long; take your seat with honor.
Read my tale with delight as a love mail
Which I'll happily tell as an autobiographer.

I am lucky to have the mind of a photographer–
Great images of my past, I can all remember.
Old, and best stories were told in our villages,
Sometimes under the moonlight's beautiful images
Where we all sat, as I am now in a foreign land.
There's a wave of joy that sweeps me back to my land
As Alice in the dreamland with a pretty garland,
So, l'm joyous to write about my motherland.

1984 I was born in Mezam Division – Santa.
I grew up as a man but never heard of Santa,
Though most people call him Santa Clause.
Not my fault; I knew in English of a Clause.
I was born to my mother as her only son,
I had a father, stepbrothers, and sister,
I grew up lonely, despite all, very handsome,
Life in my early years was sinister.

I often sought the reason I was lonely born.
Sometimes, I watched movies like James Bond
To escape mental idleness, to ease my pain.
I was born in West Africa, Cameroon,
A peaceful nation once under imperial tycoons,
Who during the scramble for African colonies,

Took great delight to rob her during harvest moon
As songs our grannies chanted as they on the loom.

Cameroon was betrothed to France and Britain,
Who did more harm and evil - it is written
In every history book, how we were smitten
By imperial greed, who betrothed Cameroon
Not for love, but saw her as a helpless buffoon.
France and Britain came to her every noon,
They dared into the hinterland or cocoon
As they set every machinery to loot at noon.

Wild Mosquitoes bit them, but they became immune.
They divided our families and also commune.
They called us demeaning names such as baboons,
They presented themselves naive like raccoons,
Bribed our forefathers with mirrors, boon,
To make them feel and fall to their doom.
They took advantage of their hospitality
And looted all with their sons in brutality.

They brought torture and heinous crimes that stink
Horrible than rotten menstrual blood in a sink.
They tricked us, beat us, killed us with deadly drinks.
Soft sweet drinks, but deadly like honey stings.
They stripped our fathers, urged them to run naked,
At gunpoint, their children watched; it was wicked.
When they refused to run, they shot them viciously,
They died in the sight of all so unsurreptitiously.

Cruel and inhumane treatment of their fathers…
Wives cried, some refused to watch any further,
They too were beaten, raped with a rifle or dagger.
They had a trained rape squad to initiate danger,
They were in their millions, walking with a swagger.
They raped indiscriminately till they did stagger.
Women's breasts were crushed or ripped with breast ripper,
Iron Spider, pains surpassing a bite from a spider.

Stripped naked, forced on Spanish donkey's back -
A wooden horse with a sharp-pointed edge back.
Some wore a scold's bridle, also called branks
Muzzled by torture or imperial cruelty or hacks.
Often, they were raped by squads of different ranks
With huge male canons like World War II tanks.
They bled but forced to stay bliss or say thanks,
They were privileged to be quad raped by gangs.

A woman was churlish if she didn't say thanks.
She was turned up-side-down with planks,
Her legs widely opened, tied to each plank.
From her genitals, she was roughly sawed or cut
And her body divided between her butts.
Some squad gangs loved the pear of anguish,
These broad daylight sadists loved to choke pear.
Women wailed and wept till they languished.

They sat others naked on a very hot iron chair,
Their flesh melted like ice as they did cheer.
Corsets were used to deform their female bodies,
Some forced to odd sex-anal, ecstasy or urges.
They invented something called blood eagle,
Our fathers were treated worse than a beagle.
They were butt-kicked to a prone position,
Their ribs cracked with knives or made incision.

Their lungs pulled sideward like a plane's wings
Despite the wailing and cries of all tribal kings.
They invented Dracula torture or impalement,
They hung you upside down for their entertainment,
Pregnant women were ripped in their abdomen,
All this, before their helpless husbands or men
At gunpoint, and in chains forced to watch,
They were denied the privilege to protest, but watch.

Many died by the Lingchi slow process.
A lingering death, slow slicing abscess,
A death by thousand horrendous cuts

Everywhere on the body, butts like guts.
Sharp bamboo heads they thrust your butts
After being hog-tied with knives on your gut.
They delighted in evil and premature burial,
They danced, sang songs of joy or memorial.

They buried one alive to be eaten up by bacteria,
They behaved strange-like beings extraterrestrial.
Though for nemesis's sake, some died of malaria,
Any cause of evil is a death criteria natural or artificial.
There was a massive graveyard for flaying,
Some were tortured by flaying or oil frying.
Days and nights, water was always kept boiling
To inflict pain on bare flesh by grilling or broiling.

All these cruelties or torture on us were for foiling
Us from defending our land, they called it roiling.
Thatched houses were burnt with Roman candles,
Parents screamed as the flames consumed or manhandled,
Them until finally, they gave the ghost, unable to handle.
Like a wicked species of animals maliciously handled.
There was no way for them to escape— escapism,
They outnumbered, killed by scaphism— cyphonism.

They killed Rudolf Douala Manga Bell;
A noble Cameroonian patriarch sent to hell,
We cannot forget this dread or his monument,
Many patriarchs died in isolation or immurement.
In a brazen bull, some died for their amusement.
Like Martin Paul Samba, bold to rebel,
Was sentenced by a military tribunal and was shot.
He died peacefully for his motherland on the spot.

Others were threatened, intimidated with strappado,
Others like Rueben Um Nyobe braved forward,
Was betrayed and assassinated in such a sorrow,
His traitors faced a fate so terrible and awkward.
I won't get into all of them; they recognize,
Even if they refuse to repent and apologize.

Never has any continent seen such barbarism,
Never did any European nation see such terrorism.

Let's forget about this; for now, let's move-on
I spoke/speak both French and English,
They named us black, savage monkeys so brutish.
So, they taught us English as a means of control.
All the same, I can speak and write English.
They later gave us another name, Anglophones,
Not because we were smart in school or did enroll,
Simply because we spoke English as a language.

Cameroon is now a nation of inter-languages
Where French is a language made official.
Very few people speak, even government officials.
I also speak French fluently, not as a Frenchman,
I speak French with an accent of a fisher of man.
Many indigenes ended up linguistically confuzzled,
They were deceived and assimilated into paternalism,
They gave up their native language, maternalism…

Trying to embrace another culture, assimilationism,
Then the task made easy for neocolonialism.
Who knows of what will be of their fate?
At gunpoint, our forefathers embraced their fate,
But today in the better times it's a matter of faith.
Some felt entrapped, but held firm to their faith,
To the path of their ancestors and demi-gods.
Who makes a difference between gods and God?

FIRST CANTO
Early Years And Inspiration

I was born on this fortunate day,
It was the month of March, at midday.
I was not there in the beginning,
But I heard the tales one blessed evening
From the mouth of my beloved mother,
Who told me my story so deepening
As only on God she was depending—
From her loins, I had no sister or brother.

She did her best as a good griot or narrator,
She was both a mother and a commentator.
Let's ride together, don't be a spectator,
I will be your only guide and narrator.
Poetry will be my language or navigator.
So after, you'll be a great solicitor.
I came forth as a lone son or child,
I was dearly loved by my grandmother.

I grew up semi-happy like one in exile,
With anxieties about life, I couldn't reconcile.
My father is Mr. John, but not the Baptist.
A man of insight who knew I would be an artist.
He spoke with the power of intelligence,
A man with a high IQ, respected for diligence.
He was known for his virtuous acquisitiveness,
An orator of unmatched wit of convincingness.

He was greatly loved for his shrewdness,
To stand for what is right with definiteness.
Always ready was he for any life coincidence,
As many in him had built trust and confidence.
He was a breed of a kind, with divine distinctiveness
Whose face glowed with happiness and exquisiteness.
His speech was well refined, with explicitness.
He had qualities of refined art with indistinctness.

Anything lacking quality or insipidness,
He would disagree with you so respectfully.
When you spoke with him, he listened carefully.
He was physically strong, also mentally.
He did nothing by chance or accidentally;
An intellectual, who did things experimentally.
He was so organized and had a trajectory,
And would never invade anyone's territory.

He's a police officer, though he loved the military,
But the military had much life of solitary.
He joined the Cameroon police force,
He was a police officer in his course.
He was an expert at settling cases on divorce,
And saved many marriages from tragedy,
He acted with dignity with laws enforced,
He advocated a more youthful labor force
Which could train youths as a brain source,
Or helped them with good education or resource.

He had a positive will, impact and reputation
In the nation Cameroon wallowing in corruption,
And posterity was endangered by its damnation.
There was no greater asset than education,
Which he encouraged every day without hesitation.
So, all he sacrificed for my tuition.

Years later, he moved to the United Nations
Where he worked for peace in all nations.
He had the mind of a great politician,
He did commentaries with the skills of a tactician.
He was always active in peace talks or negations,
And believed in diplomacy as a means of reconciliation.
War was a self-destructive form of temptation
If care was not taken to do things in moderation.

He saw that technology was leading to aberration,
He loved good technology or modernization,

Modernized society suffered from isolation,
Everyone made social media surfing an occupation.
Computers came with much joy and simulation,
Schools made some mandatory or an obligation.
A modernized world at the peak of civilization,
Yet the books say Africa is the cradle of civilization.

Though I was the lone son to my mother,
I had other brothers and sisters from another.
The roof of a polygamous home is always afire,
Never a pleasant of life for anyone to admire.
My parents' love tale at birth grew darker,
Not by the absence of light or any marker.
Things grew too complicated or harder;
A love tale of agonies, pains, and deception.

I grew up with misconceptions quite a lot
About my parents' love story or tale,
On what happened for things to fail.
As a child, I was told concealed details
My mind was still fragile to digest or inhale
Love battles between adults in hearts travail.
Time was needed to break through or prevail,
Though sometimes, I secretly will wail.

I sometimes felt lonely as one in jail
I sometimes felt terrorized with fear to fail.
Time was to speak for itself or unveil
Any secret or mystery in full detail.
Sometimes, our past is obnoxious to behold,
Some are born poor, others in a rich household.
We all have the same race to run or goal
To fight for survival till we grow old.

I wasn't born so mediocre nor rich,
Though riches sometimes define our outreach.
Why was I born alone and others in twos?
This began my inquisitiveness and infant woes.
Lone children are often given an impression.

Some people envy them for succession
As those who have been there pity their isolation,
But the truth remains unique, sometimes depression.

I had all I wanted when I growing up,
But all needs and wants couldn't make up
For the emotional void of a lone child
Which occasionally made me very shy.
Many are some in my same boat today
Born from infatuations, love tales or decay.
They may look outwardly contented,
But within them is a dread so resented.

We see how life is sometimes cruel or unfair,
Where many for love's seek or sake are where
They should not be or have been to dare.
They accept all odds, fate of agony, they bear.
Many at their infanthood are destitute aware
That life is not a bed of roses with roses,
Some are pressed to live what life imposes.
Other as prostitutes, thieves, or drug overuses.

Now you can make a start to understand
Why my childbirth back in my homeland
As a lone child brought to my mind
Solitude so hard to tell or define.
I was born from a youthful love affair,
A love affair which wasn't fair.
This is all I can say at this point or tell you.
As a child, there was nothing I could do.

I had no choice, but rather my lone fate.
I craved for brothers or sisters as playmates,
But such was never my case or equate
For childbearing cannot to mere play equate.
My parents, once lover-birds of a pair
Finally had to come to points of despair.
They had to stay away and also apart,
Though once in a while, they crossed path.

I was often too sick, sick surreptitiously,
I would see my Mum weep so expeditiously.
She would rush me from hospital to hospital for aid,
But could not find aid or help from hospital aid.
I saw the tears of single motherhood,
She was brave, fought as a lioness would
To protect and save her only son.

She would go hungry under the scorching sun,
And a lot more sacrifices for her son.
She would tarry late all nights weeping,
Stirring at me with a heart bleeding.
I can remember the anguish on her face,
She was pale, with a face like a cracked vase.
Her anguish soul seemed deprived of grace,
She was ready to seek help from any place.

We visited many shrines to find healing,
But our efforts ended up unappealing.
We visited many meetings, some native doctor—
Most of them were naïve entertainers like actors.
I was to grow with this mental pain,
Bitterness, self-pity, or anger detained.
Though born free, I was all in chains.
I needed family love and not mundane.

I grew with pain within me contained.
I sought freedom every day to attain.
When I saw little children playing around,
My pain grew, and in tears my heart abound.
Later, literature will be a catharsis,
The healing balm with poetry emphasis.
In my loneliness and withdrawn state,
I would begin to write, so started my fate.

SECOND CANTO

Education

I gradually came of tender age.
This was to be the start of a new page.
To some, it might be a truth so untrue or hard,
But this truth is from the depth of my heart.
I was not smart or brilliant in school back then,
Though education was ink to my poetic quill pen.
When my left hand could touch my right ear,
It was a great joy and celebration for me that very year.

It meant I could go to school without fear
Like everyone in their uniform wear.
Having your left hand touch your right ear
Was the fitness of a child, a sign so clear
That they were ripe for school that year.
Some parents would be happy and drink beer
To celebrate that their child was fully grown,
For that was the only measurement known.

Birth certificates to determine were not common.
So, they made noise until it was fully known,
Known by all, even to their worst enemies.
Sometimes, it provoked animosity or envies.
It was in Mbouda, a western region or city,
Of Cameroon when I began my nursery.
My nursery years were full of diversity
As we were taught to chant the rosary.

I loved being at school than at home alone,
Home loneliness made my heart groan.
I recollect acting my first drama or play,
I was five years; I won prizes for my birthday.
I was seeking a form of emotional catharsis,
I mused, and was fully coaxed in my analysis
That I was born a poet and playwright
Writing was part of me and my birthright.

My nursery school was near my Mum's workplace.
After school, I went across the road or walked
To her office and waited for her to finish.
Solitary at home made my joy to diminish.
At sunrise, we all from home vanished.
Vanished every day, every week, every term
Until the academic year itself vanished.
The good and bad days in time too vanished.

Alas! I had passed through my nursery,
It consoled me to forget my misery.
I was now ready for the next class.
The day finally came for me alas!
I attended Mbouda Primary School,
On my first day, the school was full.
My next level was called class one,
I was new in class, level, and uniform.

At first, I was glad about everyone,
But just very few, I did finally trust.
Few I trusted, with some few I did entrust.
Every pupil wore a blue top uniform,
A short nicker that made us uniformed.
Some days were unfriendly with storms,
We had to put on pullovers to keep warm.
But the muddy roads were unfriendly and frown.

They taught us English language grammar,
But I disliked it since I only loved drama.
Elementary life became more interesting
As I had enough knowledge worth trusting.
It was years of hard work at home and school
With much expectation and the whips at school.
After seven years of elementary education,
I passed my Common Entrance Examination.

I was now ready to face the post-elementary.
I had hoped for something complementary,
But it was an entire ecosystem of learning

Which prompted my interests or yearning.
Time passage later taught me many things.
New things everyday came or did spring.
My suppressed emotion developed wings
From being home-bound, enraged, and caged.

I had friends to share my seclusion or rage,
Though some friendships had terms or strings.
I hated my teacher, "Mr. Touch Your Toes,"
He loved to punish us, telling us to touch our toes.
When we bent down to touch our toes,
He used all his might to flog or lash our butts,
We cried till we felt our belly hurt through our guts.
He was trusted by the administration and parents.

We had no choice; he was our Math teacher,
He was athletic with huge dreadful features.
We nick-named him "Horrid Creatures."
When he spoke, his voice was a thunderstorm.
He had one suit which we called his uniform.
When he yelled at you, a particle of dust rose,
His mouth stretched like elastic, and his eyes
Shivered, his muscles expanded big and wild.

He was our African version of Hulk.
No student or girl would like to give him a hug.
Green leaves behind the class changed their forms
When he sneezed to avoid any deforms.
I saw him smile just once in his lifetime.
Often, he looked like a criminal without a crime.
I was soon to leave for Government Bilingual
High School Mbouda, a college multilingual.

Mr. Touch Your Toes was off my sight and way,
I could now play at free will or even fly away.
Teachers in the college did not care.
They only cared about their affair.
I was about fifteen of age, or even beyond,
I had enough friends to play with or correspond.

I will learn the good and bad habits,
We played Ali Baba and his forty bandits.

A friend compared his manhood to a python,
He bragged it was good for an Olympic marathon.
His girlfriend will beg him and even cry.
She was always in pains and feared she could die.
He mentioned the Guinness World Record
Despite the screams women in his bed did record.
He claimed his name will be written as a report,
And he will be given a huge sum as a reward.

I was not always with him in one accord.
Though we were friends, he was always bored.
He told me why girls loved him or adored,
For any girl on his bed with a dreadful testimony returned.
He had the right and perfect size to turn them on
Once they were horny, he played with their horn.
We would play hide and seek games,
Mummy and daddy, though with other aims.

He loved to play with his girlfriend only,
He argued that we could play it best if slowly.
We were all youths still in our teens,
Some of our games would be hidden scenes.
Sometimes, our lover peers or classmates
Would write love notes to their soul mates.
I learnt good and bad things from chums,
When I did wrong or right, they gave me a thumb.

They spent all night drafting love letters
For the loveliest way to express by letter writing.
The next day, they begged their soul mates' books
And sneaked the love letters in them or in their sweaters.
It made me socially accepted, felt good within,
For there were burning passions and questions within,
Though my conscience would beat me inside,
Passions and voices would be bubbling inside.

I was the kind of slow water flowing very deep.
We will bet and toss with friends for a tip.
Who was to bell the cat, or woe a new boo.
Everyone wanted to prove courageous
By attempting to show what they could do
Our conversations were always ambiguous.
What we spoke about as boys was outrageous,
Sometimes, they were obscene or contagious.

I learnt what it meant to smoke a cigarette,
We smoked before looking for a coquette.
I truly hated some of our discussions,
I knew they had dangerous repercussions
But I still enjoyed them for friendship's sake.
If I did not, they would hate me or even forsake.
We engaged in a willful concussion or fight
To test one another's strength to wrestle.

Our uniforms torn like grain under a pestle,
And our books ruffled like in a thrash nestle.
Our best subject was Human Biology.
For me, it was a new school of discovery.
Our teacher that day taught human reproduction.
We took notes, everyone in careful attention,
We made noise in class during Sociology,
I disliked it just as I did Technology.

After our Human Biology class or session,
My friends grew up being so obscene, an obsession,
For some used their grammar for possession.
Some were wealthy, with every attractive possession.
One was Richard, maybe because they were rich,
He got access to everything for outreach.
He grew in confidence and affluence,
This gave him stamina and a lot of influence.

He had the highest number of non-attendances.
He had his way in every situation or instance.
He was youngest, but was feared by instructors,

He earned the name Great Rico, mentor of mentors.
He was the dullest of all who would need a calculator
To calculate one plus one or any denominator.
He knew nothing; he had a coconut head.
A badass student, many failed or were misled.

My school grades were getting so horrible,
They weren't too deplorable or adorable.
I managed to pass from Form One to Form Two.
I knew deep within me there was much I had to do.
Good news, most of my friends passed too,
And more friends added to the queue.
My childhood solitude was now a stranger,
I had enough fun with other teenagers.

I was also very gifted in-home agriculture,
This passion will later turn to horticulture.
I hunted birds, birds that beseemed a vulture,
I set traps, caught birds, and kept them in cages.
I built bird cages at different times or stages.
My environment was becoming unfriendly,
Things needed to be done differently.
That year, 2000, I had to go to Bamenda.
Farewell, Lycée de Mbouda!

THIRD CANTO
Life In Bamenda

I grieved leaving my friends behind,
Old reminiscences wrestled in my mind.
I had to be brave with a lion's mind
To let go of youthful passions behind.
Friends are everywhere, easy to find,
I had to console myself not to be confined.
Soon, I was to meet friends of all kinds,
Some were horrible; Richard-like to say or define.

But I had to love and accept all mankind,
My feelings about my new life were mixed.
Honestly, my heart wasn't on anything fixed,
For nostalgic feelings crowded my mind.
I was to live with my maternal uncle,
I feared nothing in him like his knuckle.
He was huge like a house and very strict,
And loved to live in an isolated district.

He did not believe in anything mystic,
Though his personal life was mythic.
Stench from his armpit smelled so rustic
While he felt so handsome and romantic.
Years later, he became a true necromantic.
I sometimes thought he was sycophantic
Or even behaved more of a lunatic.
He was uneducated, more like pedantic.

One day he said he crossed the transatlantic
In his dreams without fear or panic.
He was strange of a being, so erratic,
And spoke like a cloned clown fanatic.
His love for women was a curse so sarcastic.
When he saw a girl, he went for magic.
He was as lecherous as a sparrow, always acrobatic
Though he loved many women by pragmatics.

His fate in bed was horrible and dramatic.
He believed to be romantic was to be organic.
He would learn western romance from Titanic.
Everything about him was queer or problematic.
I was not sure how to relate to him,
His whole frame was always dim or grim.
I am not sure he ever smiled in his life,
Or only smiled when tickled by his wife.

He was to introduce me to a new culture,
Eating at the table, something not my nature.
I did not like the principle so much,
But had no choice but to obey him as such.
I loved eating *achu* with my forefinger
Over and over until it was well washed,
I would chew meat and all bones squashed.
He looked at me with wild eyes, quashed.

In his presence, I ate with dignity or ethics,
I am sure he might have done bioethics.
Most often, I wished he wasn't on the table
For me to eat until I was full or disabled.
His eyes stared like a forked serpent tongue.
From plate to plate, they aimlessly swung.
I felt ashamed to eat plentiful how I would,
And only ate so little and did not feel good.

He will always be the last person to leave,
His presence always brought my heart grief.
Sometimes I pretended to be full to gain relief,
I rushed to the kitchen and hid unperceived,
Just to lick my fingers after folding my sleeve
Hoping he won't catch me and slaps release.
He suspected my conduct at one point in time,
He knew something wasn't right or in rhyme.

I stole chocolate cookies, waiting for bedtime
When I ate what I couldn't during the daytime.
One day I left the table in haste,

He had been watching my wrinkled face.
I soon vanished from his sight to the kitchen
As I ate, I had some crumbs on my chin.
I heard his footsteps like those of a cat,
I cleaned my hands and hid like a rat.

He never spoke sometimes but looked at you,
Sometimes, stared, scared, and tore you through.
You would begin to cry or even confess
Without him asking if you did transgress.
I knew that he was going to bury me alive.
I had thought about how else to survive
If he gave me lashes on my butt, forty-five,
For he always administered whips in five.

I looked left and right where I could dive
If he came closer against me like a power dive.
He looked at me, called me with his finger;
I saw on his face bitterness and danger.
Then, he retreated to the living room
As I followed like a raccoon.
On my way, I stopped in the restroom
To catch my breath before meeting my doom.

With his long finger like an abandoned broom,
I was like thread-fitted in the loom.
He ordered me down on my knees,
I went down, so scared even to sneeze.
I was already a dead man; what else to worry?
My heart was hardened, not even to say sorry.
His dark and black nose was like a horse's tail,
It looked disgusting, untidy, looking pale.

His teeth had become dark-brown,
He wore his favorite suit, filthy brown.
He was built like a baobab tree, all brawn,
His eyelids were crowded dust-brown.
His tongue was chameleon's at length,
Sometimes, he swanked of his tensile strength,

Though his wife complained about his virility,
And preferred the neighbor for his viral ability.

He thought muscles equaled bed performance,
Whereas he knew nothing about romance.
Sometimes, I heard him say he went to France
To improve his bedmatics or romance enhance.
He was so horrible, even when it came to dance.
Every night, they fought at every instance,
It was a love fight; she loved it with no chance,
But he was such barbaric that made her scream.

Even through her eyes, just at first glance,
One could tell she loved it not by chance.
Orgasm for her was a game of luck or chance,
Perhaps, with other men, it was at all circumstance.
They had dark secrets that I knew very well.
They cheated on each other with nasty a smell.
With this, I was now as confident as hell
To someday take my revenge if they did yell.

His phone rang, for the first time, he smirked,
He answered with a soft voice and jerked.
He flamboyantly walked into his bedroom
Like a thief in a trial session or courtroom.
I tried to eavesdrop his dialogue,
But heard nothing except a monologue.
He did not say a word, just a listener.
I was still down on my knees as a prisoner.

I was looking at the clock tick and tick,
He was not fast coming any time quick.
I was sure it was one of his side chicks,
Perhaps, that was why he was somehow meek.
While on my knees, I thought of a trick,
First, I thought to pretend I felt sick.
It was not going to be best or work so well,
He knew me very well and could tell
If I was sick or not by just a sense of smell.

What else could I do to get out of this hell?
My knees already; I feared they would swell.
A postman knocked and rang the doorbell.
I had already been up before he could yell,
"Go and get that parcel; it's from dell."
Once I got the parcel, I stood for a while,
Thinking of what would be my next vile.

I mustered valor to knock on his door,
My voice sounded frail and sore.
He opened the door, looked at the package,
Looked at it again and saw no damage.
I was waiting for another punishment so savage,
But he smiled at me; my heart was salvaged.
For the first time since he was born,
He wished me a happy birthday without scorn.

I said "Thanks," like a celebrity who mourned.
It was rare to hear him compliment anyone.
I pretended to be unhappy with my heart torn.
Hello, someone called loud like a truck's horn.
He rushed back into his room smiling,
I suspected something was beguiling.
Well, all I needed was my autonomy.
I shut the door and went to the balcony.

I was still culpable and somehow entrapped
As I oddly looked at the mail and unwrapped.
Even if he found out I wasn't on my knees,
At least, I would have had some good breeze.
He emerged from the room looking refreshed,
From his face, I saw his soul was afreshed.
He was gentler, with no trace of agony.
Did he see an angel from Gascony?

The sun was soon to rest and rust,
It was windy, with a damn air with dust.
He stood by me, but silent for a while,
His face was noble, neither wide nor wild.

He lifted his eyes towards the sky,
Then looked at me, "You're good guy."
He said, and adjusted his bow tie.
I didn't believe he was speaking the truth or a lie.

For him to speak as such hardly occured.
Was he truthful or just telling a lie?
He thrusted his hand into his left pocket
And pulled out his wallet, so crooked.
Can a surprise be expected from his wallet?
My eyes were tottering from his face to locket.
My eyes wandered just like my thoughts,
Not knowing if all will again be naught.

Contrary, he had me another surprise,
He counted some banknotes twice,
It was Ten Thousand Francs to be precise.
I wasn't still sure it was for me the money
Till he gave it to me like a woman horny.
My heart was sugary with milk and honey.
My heart within leaped with baffling pleasure
To believe I had such money for my leisure.

Five minutes later, pulled over a cab.
The cab driver had a reddish face cap.
The cap seemed to have had many mishaps.
He wound down the cab glass,
His eyes were like one who's taken kvass
 As if it produces mirages through a glass.
My attention was somehow divided,
I tried to be nice before things got lopsided.

He quickly pointed to the roadside,
So, my uncle knew the cab by the wayside.
He entered his room and vanished outside.
They drove off before any woe could betide.
I cared little of where he was going,
Dusk had set, the night was fast growing.
I looked at the money again and again,

I thought of what to buy, a play station game?

My emotions dangled, challenging to tame
With questions, could this be a sort of game?
I remembered I had a small bank,
I rushed to my room, with the door banged.
Suddenly, the doorbell began to ring,
Bitterness bit me within like a sting.
I ignored it at first, but it rang and rang,
I spoke to myself in Pidgin English,
"Na which kind badluck again be dis?
Why must the bell spoil my evening bliss?

It was my Auntie who was at the door ringing,
Though vexed, I feigned to be happy or singing.
She smiled and joined me to sing happy birthday,
Fear had made me forget it was my birthday.
She had genuine comforting smiles everywhere
Though I was fond of her joviality anywhere.

She gave me tender hugs like a baby,
She looked cute, but I was very shabby.
She got in, threw herself on a love seat,
Opened her bag with joy devoid of deceit,
She counted some cash and licked her finger.
Then, she paused and continued like a thinker.
I hope she won't change her mind,
My heart raced so fast, undefined.

My eyes were also counting silently
As she recounted it again quietly.
Alas! She said you could have this.
Use it for your bliss, or please!
I smiled pretentiously but graciously,
And began to thank her loquaciously.
She was a good woman, but ostentatious,
She was like a mother, so nice and precious.

When I needed something,

I knew she was capable of supplying.
Then, I'll become technically sagacious.
To hide any negative emotion or mendacious.
I knew she must be tired and well-wearied.
Her brow later grow pale, then harried,
Signs of tiredness all over her as she yawned.
I discerned she was somehow worried.

I knew she was long married,
It pained me so bad to see her worried.
She was never happy in her bedroom
Which I guessed was a war room.
I sneezed and noticed she got frightened.
She stood up and picked her bag in a deep groan.
I loved her, and she needed to be counseled,
Perhaps it would help solve her begroan.

FOURTH CANTO

P.C.H.S Mankon
Progressive Comprehensive High School Mankon Bamenda

Weeks later, I was to begin school again.
My new school was on a steep hill or plain.
Many other students came for admission,
Though I had my suspicion or opinion.
Progressive Comprehensive High School
Was my new institution or new school.
They dressed in a white shirt, long black pants,
From the dormitory, I heard some voices chant.

Their voices sounded like those of prisoners
Or tormented souls in a parish or parishioners.
I was not there for admission but also a listener.
I began making friends, one with a scrivener.
He said his father was called Pismire,
Yet I saw little in him to admire,
And truly, he was smaller than an ant.
Though as tiny as an ant, he was still relevant.

In Progressive, my friends were less aggressive,
I met good ones, some very impressive.
I hated chemistry but loved literature,
I loved poetry most due to its structure.
One could use a word to describe nature.
Our poetry class was in a hall with entablature,
Always full of delight, truth, and pleasure.
So, I fell in love with literary nomenclature.

I was confident about how to express my trauma,
It was not through grammar but drama.
There I met a man who had me branded
Not like others in the staff, a special brand.
He was my professor, Awah Nde Oliver,
A man versed in poetry, even in his liver.
He was like an arrow; poetry was his quiver.
His love for poetry would make you shiver.

His diction like the Bible, teaching like a life giver.

A man young in age, interesting in grammar
And his whole being wrapped in drama.
He was full of love and enthusiasm,
He spoke against corrupt iconoclasm,
And his speech full of wit or colloquialism.
He believed in truth, perfection, and utopianism,
And was highly praised for his vocalism,
For all he raised were direct products of vocalism.

From him, I learnt of a writer, Shakespeare,
An English playwright with no poetic fear.
I knew I would one day be one, one of such;
A writer who writes without fear and much.
He became my mentor, teacher, and coach.
I will soon learn poetry in all its approach.
We performed plays with a social broach,
For his works had a sweet euphemistic approach.
He used the stage to bring other's reproach,
Corrupt regime officials called the cockroach.

Romeo and Juliet was my favorite of all.
A tale of Romeo and Juliet in love,
A legendary tale, which by love did befall.
I began my journey as a poet or to write,
He said anyone who writes not has no life.
Then, I wrote Miss Angel to my delight.

Miss Angel was a teenage love sonnet,
A sonnet that sought love like a broad net.
Miss Angel will later become a book,
My first masterpiece or sketchbook.
Literature was soon to be my new friend,
I could now write any time with no end
As a new life beginning had opened
My past in poetics was a good blend.

I went nowhere during my weekend,

But spent time writing or making amend.
I will soon pass my Ordinary Level exams,
A state board exam with birth pangs.
I soon loved Bamenda, a lovely city,
You could easily find *achu* or anything crispy.
Life was now bringing me true happiness
As I stayed away from childish crappiness.

In high school, I specialized in literature,
Literature in English and French orature.
I was now in my late teens, nineteen,
With mastery of dramatic art acts or scenes.
Thanks to the mentorship of a radical man,
The man who did what was right for his own,
The man whose whip was his mouth.
No evil around escaped his rebuke.

FIFTH CANTO
The University Of Dschang

After high school, I was university headward.
I won many poetry contests and awards.
I went to the Dschang state University,
The city of the universe, with diversity.
This university was known for its multiversity,
Though with a lot of immorality or perversity.
I met all forms of things in this universe,
I met a He-She on campus, something averse.

A world where people live life so adverse,
A life impure to the soul, source of my heroic verse.
I wrote many university poems, such as free verse,
Not all verses were free; others were blank verses.
Well, I was literarily versed and immersed.
I became a critic of anything I saw inverse.
I enrolled into the Faculty of English Modern Letters
Where I studied literature to get even better.

I met Dr. Nkongmenec Vivian, an abettor
Who will later become a mother and a mentor.
We gave her a nickname, "Small pepper"
She was very loving, but as sharp as a shredder.
She was a woman of principle or discipline,
You dare not misbehave or cross her line.
Think twice before you smile aimlessly,
She would tongue-lash you fearlessly.

Her class was sometimes as quiet as a graveyard,
Everyone's mouth was always on guard.
When she smiled, we took advantage to chatter,
Some students would chatter, and others clatter.
Though strict, she brought us much laughter,
She was selfless towards students, no matter.
How often she did yell or batter,
Seriousness at studies was her matter.

She was a lecturer and a mother
Who taught, disciplined not to smother.
She was an outstanding subject matter
Who taught literature better or smarter
Than any feminist orator or lecturer.
Times were tough, sometimes hard times,
And made us see through texts all the times.
She taught us Charles Dicken's Hard Times!

She would make life lively all the time,
We all laugh, talk about her at break time.
Oliver and herself were once classmates,
She taught prose and poetry in all their states.
She saw the poet in me, in Miss Angel,
A poem I loved and sang as an evangel.
She introduced me to *Sons and Lovers*
By D. H Lawrence, a love tale of others.

Gertrude Morel, an unhappy mother,
Tragic heroine, whose fate brought bother.
Paul Morel and my life were alike,
Pains of unloved marriage, woeful strike.
Worse of all, the dread of emasculation
Not to fall into its pitfalls or frustration.
Paul Morel was just a universal emblem
Of broken marriages and their problem.

I was comforted with Paul's predicament,
And couldn't blame him or his ambivalent.
He struggled between two love or lovers,
His Mum and girlfriend as two lovers.
Should one love his mother deep as such,
Not to feel for other women this much?
Many are in such dilemma of emasculation
As life turns around circles of evolution
So grandiloquent in Charles Darwin's evolution
Theory or even brag of its mutation,
But fails to see the problem or frustration.

I acted Paul Morel in a stage play or drama
Just as perfect as he would in his trauma,
A recollection of woeful or powerful emotions;
Emotions long-suppressed now in explosions.
Alas! I was relieved with some theatrical motions.

Here came another beloved professor,
Kashimist A, an oralist possessor!
Professor Enongene Sone, the oralist,
Known for his Kashmistic diction or realist.
He taught me oral literature with dignity,
Made me see the flavor of oral poetry
And spoke as professor and mentor
Professor Kashim Ibrahim Tala with benignity.

Professor Kashim, a voice of orature,
A man with multifaceted wisdom of nature
Who brought life to literature in Africa.
Under them I learnt, was well nurtured.
From them, I drank proverbs like palm wine
And drank oral literature like a vine so divine.
No one sits under such great vines
And remains only leaves, they become branches.

Professor Enongene, a man of words so refined
Who spoke orature with peace of mind,
So unique in eloquence, truly one of its kind.
He was all in one, a poet of African oration
Whose redemptive word brought salvation.
His wisdom was unchangeable or unmatched,
His class was always hilarious, supercharged,
As I went home happy and literarily recharged.

He had nicknamed me poet Fabrice
As he saw poetry flow in me like a breeze.
He had foreseen far ahead into the future
That there was a poet still hidden in nature.
His words brought me bliss and breeze,
So as to say, a prince of peace!

He taught me comparative literature,
A man of all weather and temperature.

SIXTH CANTO
Born Again Experience

Everything has its own time;
Time for peace and wartime,
Time for war and peacetime.
There is no problem without a solution.
Occasionally, drawback can become a volition
Or it might push many to a locution.
In all, no problem is long-lasting,
But every solution can be everlasting.

Not everybody who smiles is happy,
Don't be harsh when people speak snappy,
They have inter-struggles and pains,
They are straining with life's woes or strains.
Such was my case, a nocturnal cry,
I sometimes felt unseen creatures by.
Most about every night in my sleep,
My soul would wail bitterly or weep.

Unknown to me were mysterious creatures,
With vicious appearances or features.
They would visit me with superpowers
To oppress me during odd night hours.
I knew something was not right,
But thought it was life alright.
I knew nothing about the metaphysical,
And believed little in the mystical.

Every morning, my strength was drained,
I felt as though I was beaten and chained.
I was confident, but not too ascertained
To tell or tell this mystery unexplained.
At one point, I thought life had no use,
Man was born to suffer or be abused.
Outwardly, I was healthy and strong,
But inwardly, I knew something was wrong.

My mind thought of Joseph Conrad
In his book, Heart of Darkness.
I felt I needed an intimate comrade
To share my burden, pains, and happiness.
Art was good, a catharsis or purgation,
But it couldn't help my negative emotion.
I even lost the desire for poetry or arts,
I felt my life falling in bits or parts.

I was depressed with a broken heart,
And all I did was by fits and starts.
Night was becoming very dreadful or scary,
Everything seemed strange and arbitrary.
I had little knowledge of what to do,
Life was really useless and screwed.
I had all I needed for my happiness,
But feared the unknown ghastliness.

I could only think about death,
Though physically, I was in good health.
Nobody would accept my soul was haunted,
My visage looked healthy to be daunted.
A friend of mine was demon-possessed,
She'd been so assertive and obsessed.
I was still naïve as to what this all meant,
So I went to watch this unfaithful event.

Like Moses in the burning bush,
I didn't see there was a divine push.
After seeing the deliverance for hours,
I began to realize they are invisible powers.
I refused to go back to my student apartment,
I needed prayers and was ready for any assent.
It was already late; the Pastor was tired,
But I won't go even if I was fired.
His name was Francis, the evangelist.
He was anointed, educated, and pragmatist.

The deliverance I watched as so abstruse,

I saw the danger of life so free or loose.
There are many meanings to freedom;
Physical freedom and spiritual kingdom.
One can be physically healthy and free,
But spiritually, he is in bondage or unfree.
This knowledge was new to me, I must agree.
A new form of paradigm change or shift,
I recalled some poets like Jonathan swift,
A Tale of a Tub, betterment of humanity
And standing to fight for everyone's liberty.

Now I see why some poets are for romanticism,
Others metaphysical or for mysticism.
I will soon discover a new source or text,
This text, called Bible to be read in context.
I am not sure when last I heard of the Bible,
A book that made my life later stable.
I was about twenty-two years old or of age,
Hearing of the Bible was a test so strange.
I was raised a Christian or in-home Christ-like
Instead, I grew up learning to hunt a shrike.
This might sound ludicrous or very ridiculous.
More than anything else, I had to be meticulous
To meet someone I never heard of Jesus!
I only know he came to die for us,
And he came to save us from our lust or loss.
Was he a metaphysical poet? I mused.

Hearing he died for me made me amused.
Why must one die for me, I was confused.
I finally got a Bible and decided to peruse,
I perused it over and over as an autobiography.
I was looking for poetic diction or orthography.
I loved the book of proverbs, not its phonography.
I was searching with my mind, not with my heart,
And for the treason why man is deep in God's heart.

That's why it was difficult and very hard
To comprehend these sacred mysteries

Which were beyond literary masteries
To understand without the Holy Spirit is very hard.
Evangelist Francis became my mentor
Who taught me the Bible, mine instructor.
I then realized that Christ was so real,
And was ready to show himself or even heal.

He lived thousand years before I was born,
His word was solid and firm as a unicorn
While he lived, he was abused and scorned,
They crucified him with a crown of thorns,
And he rose in creation as our firstborn.
He was beaten, and all his garments were torn.
Yet men were courageous to gamble his garments,
Men were courageous to thrust vinegar into his throat.

Like Nicodemus, I was finally born again,
I accepted Jesus as I heard he was slain,
Slain as a lamb, and his death was not in vain,
But defeated Satan and brought humanity gain.
In him was life, and this life our divine light.
He was now a divine spirit, his light so bright.
The light that shineth in the paths of men
That they who embrace can never again live in the dark.

He was superior to all the poets and writers,
He will give you anything, just be waiters,
He is superior to all medics as he heals
Without laboratories, tablets, injections, or syringes.
He is the rock of ages who was, is, and is to come
He was present before every history ever came
Waiters of his presence, and by his grace,
We will package your life to be in place.

SEVENTH CANTO
Book And Prophecies

I was still naïve and foolish.
I couldn't stop thinking ghoulish.
My love for poetry was in decline.
My passion for Jesus did incline.
I wanted to know more about him,
I wanted to know more about El-Elohim.
I craved to some of the wonders with him,
I wanted to know the price to follow him.

If Jesus was more than William Shakespeare,
Then, I should love him without fear.
If Jesus was more than William Carlos William,
Then, I should love him more than a trillion.
If Jesus was more than T. S Eliot,
Then, I should love him like an idiot.
If Jesus was more than Robert Frost,
Then, I should love him, preach to the lost.

If Jesus was more than Gwendolyn Brooks,
Then, I should love him, read his books.
If Jesus was more than Emily Dickenson,
Then, I should love him, proud to be his son.
If Jesus was more than Gertrude Stein,
Then, I should love him who had no stain.
If Jesus was more than William Blake,
Then, I should love him; he wasn't fake.

If Jesus was more than Robert Burns,
Then, I should love him without any concerns.
If Jesus was more than Walt Whitman,
Then, I should love him; he wasn't a white man.
If Jesus was more than William Butler Yeats,
Then, I should love him; he never suffered defeat.
If Jesus was more than Adrienne Rich,
Then, I should love him; he will make me rich.

If Jesus was more than Patricia Lockwood,
Then, I should love him; he is ever good.
My new life in Christ was apparent,
Friends saw it as a new life, so transparent.
The feelings were mixed, paradoxical,
Some saw my life as methodical,
To others, I was brainwashed by radicals
Of born-again gospel enthusiasts or preachers.

Religious sects were rampant, with many teachers,
Some of them were genuine, others fake,
Other's preached for fame and money's sake.
Many began to alienate themselves completely,
They formed gossip groups to chatter privately.
I was mocked; they said all kinds of things,
They incriminated and nicknamed me all kinds names,
I stopped socials gatherings and cut some strings.

I suffered rejection and peer persecution,
But this was part of my journey to resurrection.
There is no resurrection without crucifixion.
I was rudely ready for my crucifixion.
Then, it was apparent we could fight evil spirits,
Not with might, but with the Holy Spirit
In the name of Jesus that was all potent,
To disarm the enemies of light or opponent.

I learnt not to wrestle against flesh and blood
As I prayed for hours till my body did flood.
I was confident to sleep peacefully
As his rod or staff comforted me gracefully.
When evil spirits came into my dream to attack,
I called the name of Jesus to nullify any setback.
The name of Jesus worked, it worked wonders,
There was no doubt, nothing to again wander.

Sometimes, I prayed with a voice of thunder
Since I had learnt some spiritual warfare
Which had improved my life and welfare.

I would struggle with my faith and studies
To reconcile Philosophy and my hobbies.
I was now in Christ, a new creation,
Narrow is the way, and broad is to damnation.
Everything wasn't good for my consumption.

Was poetry evil before God or sinful?
I had a lot of poems, let's say binful.
I loved Jesus; I also loved poetry writing,
Both game pleasures were exciting.
Songs of Solomon became my consolation
That gave me relief in all my desolation.
If Songs of Solomon was in the Bible too,
It means Jesus loves drama and poetry too.

I talked with many, to hear their views,
They sounded confused in their reviews.
It was a transitional dilemma in my growth,
My heart was made up under a solemn troth.
To be faithful to him and be exemplary,
I was still to mature from this rudimentary.

Jesus does not decrease you; he increases you,
He had a plan, a plan to see me through
This sinful world, and give me the true
Wisdom from above that was pure or new.
The Bible was going to be my breakthrough
In poetry or art with which to get through.
It gave me a real and even world view
Of life, sin, mortality, and racism so untrue.

Men torture others; they try to subdue,
They enact laws, then, try to push them through.
One night, I slept and had a dream.
From afar, I did see a bright beam.
People were all aligned with eagerness,
They were like the sand in the wilderness.
Suddenly, they began to fight and fight.
I was wondering what the serious fight was about.

They were purposeful in nature, the fights,
They fought like well-trained knights,
All they wanted was to read my books.
They loved my books and also my looks.
They were ready to get them by hooks,
They were prepared to get them as crooks
They were ready to get them for textbooks.
Then, I saw God like in the Bible's books.

I woke up from this dream in the morning,
It was a prophecy; it was a forewarning.
I needed to start work so hard, preparing,
I knew I had a future so bright and adorning.
I had another dream; the sick were healed,
As I prayed for them, so real to conceal.
Jesus appeared to me, laid his hand on my head,
Washed my feet, hands, ears, and broke bread.

He was real, white light as the Godhead
The first born of every creation, he's, our head.
His garment, white, spotless without a wrinkle.
So loving, his blood did speak and sprinkle,
His countenance, bright and so twinkled.
His light in my soul did shine and tinkle.
His presence surpassed all earthly knowledge
I wished it wasn't a dream; I must acknowledge.

With two or more witnesses, truth is established,
What is genuinely from above can't just vanish.
That which he begins, he will finish.
His presence daily I longed and famished.
My fears and anxiety were banished,
My poetic quill was divinely brandished.
I could now write poetry again as I wished,
Not just by might, but by divine grace lavished.

Finally came a futuristic word of prophecy,
Books I will write with poetic constancy,

A creative style of verse drama consistency
For his life and sacrifices know consistency.
Oh anytime anyone connects to this current,
There is grace not to fear any torrent,
You enter into a genuine realm of excellence
And possess wisdom only from above.

EIGHTH CANTO
Voyage To America Prophecies

Only in the news, I knew of America,
I was born and bred in Cameroon, Africa.
Despite my skills and writing talent,
I needed benevolent men who won't relent.
Regrettably, we had men of self-ego
Whom one could hear from afar echo.
Metaphysical poetry was to become my credo
As I will see things differently, even as Plato.

Finally came my day of graduation,
I learnt much during my university education.
The university was also my spiritual formation,
Though it was a rigid transformation.
I was overwhelmed with much anxiety,
For I knew how corrupt the culture or society
From which I was, Cameroon as a nation,
Corruption was beyond human imagination.

Many graduates were in economic isolation
With degrees, but no jobs for their consolation.
With literature, I was not sure of what to do,
Many of my classmates weren't sure too.
Perhaps pick up a job in one school or college,
The wages were too low to teach in a college.
Well, I had no choice as a graduate.
Gradually, I was becoming dispassionate.

Life was not fair; many things inadequate,
Corruption in Cameroon was inappropriate,
The national language of postgraduates.
I was now in Yaoundé the political capital,
A beautiful city, with the petty municipals.
I got a job as an English Language instructor.
I taught with fervor, like a musical conductor
Hoping to many I'll be a good mentor.

I was twenty-three years old or of age,
I was the youngest in class, how strange!
The youngest of all students whom I taught,
You can imagine other's feelings or thoughts.
To have a young instructor or teacher,
Some students had huge muscles or features,
Others, taller than me twice or even thrice,
Some were rough, disrespectful, others nice.

I thought of David and Goliath in battle,
I had to fight for my job or my only castle.
The end of the day brought me more solace,
I tried to remain brave and divinely graced.
I knew I had no strength if not of divine grace,
That fueled my hope to keep up with the race.
I traveled to Kumba, Southwest Province,
God is always faithful in his providence.

I went to see my mother at work, in taxation,
My thoughts were trapped, always in nutation.
I loved poetry, Jesus but needed food to eat,
I know Jesus could provide me food or meat.
I was worried about how to stand on my feet,
I did not just want to accept failure or defeat.
One evening we went for a retreat
In Kumba, opposite the main market street.

Many people came from afar, new faces I did meet.
It was a small church with excessive heat.
The structure was of plank, still incomplete.
I entered with my blue tie and black suit.
Everybody looked holy in their seat,
They were all well dressed, looking so neat.
The walls were plank, the floor concrete.
People worshipped as if trying to compete.

Ushers at the door did welcome and greet,
Church bulbs were brown and obsolete.
Though one could see some great feat,

I was still new there and very discreet.
I went far behind, alone in the backseat,
Where I could see everyone or any deceit.
The choir was anointed as they sang
In a few minutes, my limitations also sank.

I felt as standing before Jesus' feet
Because my joy and peace were complete.
Every second in his presence was sweet,
The fragrance of his presence was noble,
Our Prince of Peace, this kind and humble!
The Pastor was a preacher, called a seer.
When he sang, his voice was like a lyre,
When he prayed, your prayer disappeared.

He was louder than a million speakers,
Everywhere in the world, you could hear.
His voice sometimes sounded like a fanfare,
People would forget their problems or despair
Just to be attentive in church or everywhere.
He would begin to pray in tongues or swear
With his head lifted to the heavens as a deer
For his parishioners held him in an esteem so dear.

It was not strange, but it was somehow rare
How people wanted help in their affairs.
It was hilarious in there, Croix de Guerre…
I wasn't sure of what was to happen next,
I was still perplexed, my heart somehow vexed.
I was at a point very timid and complexed
With strange feelings to verbally express
In there then, I knew not which prayer to press.

In my heart was a burning prayer request
For God to give me fulfillment or rest.
I was between depressed and impressed,
I must confess my heartbeat with unrest.
Someone yelled, Holy Ghost arrest,
A lady had fallen; she was possessed.

She began to yell with much distress,
And even attempted to get undressed.

'Thus sayeth the Lord…' the Pastor blasted
In a series of prophecies, it long lasted.
He walked in the crowd with a small vest,
His eyes raced with grace on a recessed,
He was calm with thoughts unexpressed.
His thoughts so compressed, were redressed.
He looked at me steadily so decompressed,
Then my eyes fixed on him half a feared.

He called me, with a voice now modest,
He called me by my name; I must truly attest.
He didn't know me; I was just a guest.
How could he have known me by guess?
I stood up with a heart well readiest,
Ready to gulp in his prophecy or ingest.
The church was calm, everything at rest.
He came closer; we were standing abreast.

Prophecy began to flow like a river,
A prophecy that would change my life forever.
He asked me to play the American DV Lottery.
This would open my doors to leave Africa,
For my destiny was awaited in America.
His words were fragile like pottery,
For they sounded like real flattery,
But it was a turning point for a new discovery.

He said, there are books I will write,
As if he looked into my heart to write.
The stories I intended began hitting my mind,
And a thousand and one thoughts on my mind.
I'll be known as a great poet or playwright,
Then in the Lord, my joy will be a delight.
He said much; it was all true and right,
I perceived in me a future truly bright.

NINTH CANTO
Preparation To Leave Cameroon

I knew little about the American DV Lottery,
I was a novice with no mastery.
Something I didn't fully understand or know,
Where was I to begin the process or undergo?
Was it just a charismatic drama or show
Since many churches had fallen so low?
Others used prophecies as means to rich grow,
Especially as they had become commercial goods.

I spent days and nights to contemplate,
I had no choice in life as a postgraduate.
Religion was fast becoming a business
Where false seers preached with conciseness.
In the days of old, many loved the apostolate,
But now, everybody wanted to be a seer.
Others so-called forensic seers to desolate,
Would frighten you with words so disconsolate.

Some will close their eyes, nod their heads
As one who had eaten pepper or bitter herbs.
We had so many, but all claimed to be true,
Some said they could give you a breakthrough
In any area of life, marriage, or business,
Though as poor as a rat in the wilderness.
It did not act so quick or with swiftness,
Though sometimes, I was urged by blitheness.

My thoughts revolved back to my dreams,
My life came back to me in all its extremes.
Cameroon was ruled by a rotten regime
Which ruled for their bellies' desire or dream.
I fought with these thoughts for weeks,
Swindlers had many ways or techniques.
I even forgot the name he gave in his prophecy,
But I remembered just America or overseas.

In the midst of this confuzzled cacophony,
I went to my Bible; there was a paper piece
I wrote it down as he did say or release.
Once I found the paper, I was at peace
As though it had spoken to me with ease.
Why not give it a try? I thought hesitantly.
I took a bike and went to town reluctantly,
For that wasn't the plan I had instantly.

I didn't even know where to go or start.
The bike man was a man of good heart.
He was as humble as death, very smart.
Perhaps a seer too who read my heart
And said, "Why not play the American DV Lottery?"
Then, we drove off for fear of robbery.
He too was frustrated with jobbery
As he drove expertly on the roads watery.

He had all the degrees to be desired,
But there were no jobs to be hired.
He even shed tears, a lawyer so aspired,
Whose dreams went down the mire.
He worked hard to earn money or acquire
So that he too would leave Cameroon.
He was skinny, jaws like a balloon.
If I can regurgitate, it was early June.

He too was born from a very low commune,
And by struggle, he learned to be immune.
He was scholarly, well-educated, and attuned.
Outwardly, one would think he was a buffoon
As he talked alone to himself every noon.
Despite all, he still made himself a boon
Who believed in divine intervention that soon
Many will be surprised to find their doom.
He knew the town more than I did,
He had no moral flaw; he was splendid.
He was well spoken of by his deeds,
He was never one of the booty bandits,

A well-respected husband by his Judith.
He was ready to make sacrifices forthwith.
I discerned he needed some help indeed,
And I was ready to help if only he agreed.

He worked hard for his family to feed,
He sacrificed for other's needs.
He was one of a kind, a new breed.
We finally got to a shop down-town,
We met a man who looked like a clown.
We greeted him and looked around,
He smiled at us; his teeth were all brown,
He looked like one with a mental breakdown.

Just like most Cameroonians beaten down
By corrupt systems, he was cracked down.
He looked at me and asked me a question,
"Do you know you're American in question?"
I was shocked, but not really surprised,
Though it was more like a surmised.
Was he too a seer disguised?
Why did everyone so prophesied?

He read my mind for a while and advised,
"Play the DV, but there is a price."
I knew traveling was heaven's decision,
My doubts were entirely in my possession.
I could choose to believe or disbelieve,
I knew my fate was a flash in brief.
"How can I help you before my shutdown?"
Darkness was coming, night melting down.
"What is a DV, give me a quick rundown,"
I requested as a child in a playground.

"You only need to pay two thousand fee,
I will play it for you, yes, I mean free,"
He replied, and asked my photo identity,
He took it, looked at it with much intensity.
His facial expression with such immensity,

Triggered on my mind thoughts of rarity.

What did he see on my card?
He looked at my ID as though a scorecard.
Despite all, he kept typing hard,
Only the keyboard was heard blowing hard.
He entered my information in the computer,
He was faster than a supercomputer.
He was so focused, needed no intruder,
Though I still looked over his shoulder.

In no time, he was finished.
Congratulations, he said in a patois Yiddish!
Dusk was now fully gone or diminished,
Darkness was darker than darkness.
The streets were calm, everywhere blackness.
Remember me, he spoke with boldness,
You are light, so bright in abstractness.
You will shine, but not without sadness.

Who was this man, I was even confuzzled!
Everything about America was a puzzle.
Why all the prophecies or words in riddles?
He took a bottle of juice and guzzled,
It was a big bottle, but was able to nuzzle.
I was totally bewildered, paused, and baffled.
I looked at the bike man; he was frazzled.
I was eaten up by compassion for him.

He had much to say, but was humbled,
His countenance was pale and grimed.
With many questions and worries
Running on his face with none to address.
Once we vanished into the dark street,
I gave him money, but he refused
I urged him for heaven's sake, and so entreat,
He was adamant, and for a long time, bemused.

TENTH CANTO
Rue De La Joie

Months went by, and had forgotten,
Life was bleak for the downtrodden.
Girls had doctorate degrees in prostitution,
They had a nickname, "Ashawo Association,"
They dressed tastefully for attraction.
Some were young, entrapped in destitution.
Some had no breasts, nothing to admire,
For every substance in them sapped like tire.

Their job and assignment, to satisfy men's desire
In exchange for money or food distribution.
They assembled in «Rue de la Joie «constitution,
They had laws and by-laws for all resolutions.
Every 'Ashawo' abided by these instructions.
They had *Njangi* monthly contributions,
Anyone who failed suffered execution
Through breast ironing or sex excruciation.

Figging was a punitive or retaliatory substitution,
New *Ashawo* suffered heavy persecution,
They faced rigorous *Ashawo* prosecution.
Every girls' mind went through dilution
By following strict codes of prostitution.
There was always a form of retribution,
Only older ones, experts got restitutions,
Younger ones double-worked for absolution.

You had to learn their code with elocution
By complying with some magical ablution.
Some were wild and spoke in circumlocution,
Their words were equipotent to electrocution.
They had the power of seduction and dissolution,
They were the *femmes fatales* with manipulation,
They were famous and known for attribution,
Some handled big loads to the diminution.

"Garri boys" had *Ashawo* girls still in evolution.
Once an expert, they had the power of devolution.
Some were ripped, raped in anticipation,
Some went through convoluted evolution,
Others through vicious and hellish ovulation,
Some suffered from severe or acute involution.
They fought over proceeds maldistribution
Sometimes due to lack of communication.

They were uneducated from their circumlocution,
A survival game, a game of co-evolution
Where others tried by all means or comminution
To reduce others to the point of irresolution.
The strongest ones always won by allocation
Life is a mystery not to jump to a conclusion.
Don't judge; learn to love all in every situation
Don't rejoice if yours is better, others in confusion.

We sometimes laugh, make of hate a diffusion
Or make other's misery a fusion of illusion.
She was an orphan, tossed by the wind of seclusion,
She was forced into prostitution by delusion,
She had no choice but to accept this collusion.
Thereafter, she would wail or weep in disillusion,
She was overworked, sometimes in contusion,
But it was the only condition for inclusion.

She had to prove herself right or face exclusion,
Twice she passed out and was given a transfusion.
An older man once came to her in allusion,
He promised her heaven and earth in profusion.
She was under-age, still undergoing maturation,
Not knowing visit lines of prostitution
He only cared for burning sensual urge or erection.
She passed out again but had no reperfusion.

He looked like a tormented ghost or he-goat,
Though rich, his best cloth was a raincoat,
His belly was of clay; he was a politician.

He was shameless, a delusion tactician
Who embezzled state funds like magicians
And used virgin blood for evil rituals.
He had killed many innocent individuals,
He loved young blood, and paid residuals.

His best friend was called a businessman,
He had money, but looked like a mailman,
He too was unashamed with an installment plan
To pay any girl with a good attention span.
They had a clique; it was called U.S.A fan
With the credo of young blood for evil power.
They loved girls with no brainpower
They would use or abuse her woman-power.

They were wild boars with hostile taste,
And loved impact play or pearl necklace.
They never loved the expert prostitutes.
Their strong customers were the young initiates.
Worst of all, they paid the hard booty,
But only the old expert mentor prostitutes
Enjoyed the booty while the young converts
Got their immature kola nuts scattered.

ELEVENTH CANTO
Diversity Visa Results

I had just finished eating my Turkey
When an email came in from Kentucky.
What the heck is Kentucky? I mused!
Was it a scam or what? I was confused!
At first, I ignored the email and hissed,
I was having a bad time, making me pissed.
I had just read part of the mail, not all.
I was once scam-preyed, not a second fall!

I had to continue my daily routine,
My best hobby was learning new cuisine.
Well—a hungry man is an angry man.
I wrestled with omelet in the frying pan,
You know men; I tasted salt ten times,
I will add more oil, more flame sometimes.
My stomach was wailing and waiting,
Saliva and my tongue were already mating.

I remembered my thoughts also debating
If I should take it off or add more heating.
My mind paused and went back to the email.
I blamed myself for not reading the detail.
I weighed its possibility on a mental scale,
Was it a scam email to get me into jail?
Omelet was ready, a sweet savor I did inhale.
It is better to eat a good meal before jail.

I ate like a wild beast at a dinner feast
Or like a criminal chased by the police.
I finished eating and went to the text.
It was a surprise, though not perplexed.
It came to heal me from being vexed.
If the email I thought scam or complexed,
It was the store man I met that night.
His text was full of light and delight.

He confirmed the email quite alright,
This stirred me up; passion it did ignite.
I went back to the email with zeal,
I read it carefully for anything concealed.
It was from a place called Kentucky,
I almost deleted the email; I was lucky
I called the store man; who is Kentucky?

He laughed with a sharp voice so bucky,
He wasn't as thin as I was; he was bulky.
He guffawed so ludicrously as if mocking,
Why mock me, what was shocking?
I only asked a question which was choking.
Time was ticking and fast clocking
As he laughed like one in the door knocking,
Many questions in my mind hitting.

I pretended to join him, as I giggled,
Was my question so silly or squiggled?
I thought of turning him off my phone,
But had he something to say unknown?
Kentucky is one of the American states,
The Diversity Visa, by the Department of State,
Allows 55.000 immigrants into the United States
Though I was ignorant on issues of the States.

"You are one of them, no doubt nor debate.
Bless heaven; you're blessed for this fate.
Not everyone had such a lucky fortune,
Let this fortune not become a misfortune."
He hanged up before I could say a word…
I was nervous; I even missed my password,
The second time, I got it right,
I was so happy and couldn't sleep that night.

I was already seeing myself in America,
But was it going to be like Africa
Where I could eat plum and cassava?
I loved fruits; my best was guava.

My heart smiled; my heart jiggled.
My facial expression was like ticked.
Was America like my little village?
Could I know everyone there by name or visage?

My Mum learnt of this great news,
I told her my story; she was amused.
Oh, how naïve I was at that time!
Naivety, of course, wasn't any crime.
I consoled myself, tried to think smart.
I couldn't wait to leave or depart,
For there were a thousand and one thoughts
From Cameroon to give my life a new start.
Being informed was just a story in part.

What was the journey going to cost?
I had no idea; I was again lost.
I had never been out of Cameroon.
Mentally, I traveled to America that noon
Though I didn't know where it was found.
I made the store man my best friend
Since he knew what to do till the end.

Cameroonians loved beer or strong drinks,
A man is only as strong as what he thinks.
I bought two crates of beer, King Beer,
And went to his shop, he drank it there.
He was the owner and drank without fear.
When he was drunk, he would tell any affair.
Life had mistreated him in a way so unfair,
He told me his life story, his despair.

I nodded to show him I honestly did care.
All I wanted was to get ready or prepare
To leave Cameroon and become a millionaire.
I heard people talk of the American dream,
Did every American have the same dream?
I was glad to live the dream so supreme.
There were many steps to follow

To meet the deadline to avoid any sorrow.

First step, submit an application form
And wait to be notified or informed.
Second step, selection of applicants,
Only a few were selected, I mean Africans.
Third step, what to do once selected,
Not everyone selected was connected.
Fourth step, qualification confirmation,
This is that step where some become unlucky.

Must have high school education,
Or must have two years of a profession.
Fifth step, immigrant visa application –
Must fill form DS-260 for consideration.
Sixth step, submit supporting documentation
To show eligibility or qualification.
Seventh step, interview preparation.
Notify you after DS-260 form evaluation.

Eighth step, review interview instructions,
Schedule, complete a medical examination.
Ninth step, review of applicant's interview
Who must attend, how, and in what view?
Tenth step, what to do after the interview,
Visa acceptance or denial in that review.
Before he finished the tenth requirement,
My brain was far into many acquirements.

I thought it was leaving a village to the other,
Where you go and pay your fare, no bother.
This means spending millions on this journey,
Little did I know it was more than a tourney.
He was relaxed, drinking his crate of beer.
My heart was as heavy as that of King Lear.
He yelled, "Are you still with me here?"
"Yes," I replied. "I am here to hear."

He said, "Go and wait for the consular.

I will be with you, your trusted counselor."
I went home, knowing I had a councilor.
This was when I knew the importance of a mentor.
Months went by, either by accident
Or not, but I can't forget that incident.
From someone unknown, I had a ring,
His voice was like a stone from a sling.

He so mispronounced all my names
As one whose tongue was not circumcised.
At least, he tried to be sure and precise,
I was not sure of his true intention or aims.
I listened so patiently, and as a patient
If it was a scammer or sorbefacient.
I responded with a positive mindset,
Though my mind was doubting or preset.

He was another heavenly one, God sent,
Who got my DV Lottery or package
Wrongly sent to him, well packaged.
Such a grave mistake from the consulate?
It was hard for me to think or regurgitate.
I trembled within, in a deficient state.
What next? Were we in different states?
He opted to bring the DV documents.

I waited for him, with some emolument,
He was of noble heart to compliment.
Finally, there he came, dressed so opulent
Who was he with such a heavenly deed?
He promised to come, and came indeed.
He came to deliver me the document,
He spoke little like a bereaved monument,
For I counted his words at every moment.

They were few, very few to say absolument.
He dressed in affluence and gold,
He was young and at the same time old.
His mind was peaceful and bold,

The weather was icy, but he wasn't cold,
He was a mystery I still couldn't unfold.
He was young, old and had two-fold,
I kept hard my feelings not to unfold.

Of personality to which none knew,
Except for him or the wind that blew!
He said, "You have books to write,
You will write them by day or night.
Jobs' trials shall befall you all right,
But be cheerful, it will be alright."
These words were strong in my heart,
His speech was seasoned and downright.

His eyes glowed like a floodlight,
He was happy, much with joyous delight.
He stood up and disappeared in the darkness
After bidding me farewell with much happiness.
I was left alone, glad but much perplexed,
Fortune on my life was golden, not hexed.
I was now aware of the awaited unwritten text
That Jesus is the author of our hidden texts.

TWELFTH CANTO
Upon Arrival In America

On March 3rd, 2010, I arrived here,
It was the coldest part of the year.
I later learnt it was called Winter,
A memorial time I did finally enter.
Winter should mean a time for wind,
Not when you are frozen to a dustbin.
All the same, I had made it well,
A journey I knew not I could foretell.

Snow was everywhere, like salt,
Drivers would drive and stop or halt,
They would wait for pedestrians to cross over,
Then they patiently and graciously drive over.
This was a new world for me altogether,
For in my country all would hit over.
Drivers seemed so kind in all weather.
They stopped, some with chairs leather.

I looked at my time; it was about noon.
Then I thought of my nation, Cameroon.
Drivers would hit you, knock you down,
If ever you crossed the road like a clown
For even the law keepers like a clown,
No one would care; it was laissez-faire.
Everyone minded their business or affair,
For if you don't, you would become a trade fair.

I was told I was in a state called Maryland.
For about a week, I kept pronouncing merryland.
Dulles International was where I did land.
The name was not important as joy inside.
I was picked up by my uncle where he did reside.
How big was America or how wide?
If Maryland was part of America,
I did not mind; I was no longer in Africa!

Maryland was the African capital city
Where Africans lived in solidarity.
Some owned properties in propinquity,
Some lived happily in tranquility,
Others still behaved the same, always guilty;
Guilty of two things: excessive drinking
And always late for everything or meeting
Just like our hours behind-scheduled meetings.

You knew an African from his thinking,
Not because they were stinking,
But from his lifestyle or even likings.
Some looked like rescued slaves from sinking,
Some ate much, but all the time shrinking.
When I saw this, I began again rethinking.
All what you see glittering or blinking
Is not gold. Gold can glitter while stinking.

Lecherous ones spent aimless days winking,
Especially after heavy boozing or drinking.
I had my own worries to be thinking,
Not wasting time on what others were singing.
Most Africans had funny a mentality
To come and rescue America's destiny.
Some had great personality
Who understood the true American reality.

America was a place of mixed morality,
Some believed mortality or spirituality,
Others in hospitality and neutrality.
America, a land of every given opportunity
For everyone, race of diverse nationality.
I met people of all nationality in one locality,
Then I saw a place of freedom for everybody.
Some races worked together in solidarity.

I saw some youths so full of vitality
Who bragged of gender change or sexuality.
I heard the word called homosexuality,

A common truth of American society.
At one point, I was full of anxiety,
I saw some morality as an abnormality.
Freedom gave freedom to promiscuity.
Anything given in excess exceeds morality.

Women could be naked in public in totality,
Of course, I mean people of the right mentality.
Life wasn't secret, nothing as confidentiality -
Feminism was the main actuality
Where women protested against men's brutality.
To some, feminism was the truth of duality,
But a right every woman without formality
Should live freely without constrained formality.

Women chanted the right to vote and sensuality,
For equal rights, rights without any partiality.
I saw a determination with one tonality,
A tonality so fierce and able for a lethality.
I understood it with some superficiality,
Though I knew well of some triviality
Which some lived freely with animality.
Others lived freely with hate and animosity
And amazed protest in a manner of congeniality
With all voices as one in all municipality.

One evening, I went to Maryland University,
I was strolling for sightseeing or modality
I looked at its building, praised its generality.
Girls almost nude, as if observing legality,
Immorality seemed a form of practicality,
And I began to question, freedom or bestiality?

Students alike shared the same commonality,
Commonality which I saw with irrationality.
Many loved such controversy or unreality,
And lived an immoral life of dimensionality.
Some called it freedom and liberality.
America was a melting pot of osmolarity

Where everything was possible with artificiality.
Must humans in God's image be such animalists?

I was greeted with gladness and cordiality,
A cordiality in which I was as territoriality.
Food was wasted, no care for fragility.
What I saw not strange was bisexuality,
Bisexuality in a manner of impersonality.
This was something worth much criticality,
Not worth being bragged of in its theatricality
Like Sodom or Gomorra, no substantiality.

And everyone I saw had some geniality.
I couldn't underestimate the rate of suicidality,
Which was real, common with much factuality
Some lived reality daily in virtuality,
Or lived daily virtuality with eventuality
That was America for me, much carnality.
America, great but suffered from amorality
With outward amorality through joviality.

I saw champions of immorality in sodality
Some were carnal, less infested by immateriality.
Things fell apart, the reality of most nuptiality.
Even villagers behaved as though from rurality.
America had fallen from its original conceptuality,
A lack of its real identity, a cultural malady.
America preached freedom, but not its gravity,
Many lived a life of vanity with such insanity.

What a freedom! What an error! What a fallacy!
Freedom, error, fallacy leading to calamity.
Some behaved like one devoid of proper sanity
Or people of sanity, but still in moral depravity.
Mass shootings, racism, or gross inhumanity,
Police kneel-killing, racism or broad profanity.
Sin, sin, sin, sin, has its mortal wages or salary.
America had so sinned and fallen short of divine mercy.

THIRTEENTH CANTO
New York City

It was my first time in New York City.
It had many banks, one of which was Citi.
I met a crowd, so huge, never seen before,
I saw many tourists who came to explore.
People were as many as ants lined up for war,
Some walked in ones, twos, threes, or fours.
I heard a thundering noise for sure,
A noise just like that of a flying plane.

My eyes raced, looking for it again and again,
I looked at the sky, but with a sight in vain.
It was the sound of a passenger train,
It made me look so naïve. Let me explain -
My ears were still novice, still untrained.
I thought this noise was from an airplane
In Africa, such noise made us hunt the sky,
We hunted with our eyes without being shy.

Whenever our eyes searched and found it,
We yelled and waved joyfully at it
As the plane we called beautiful as it flew by.
I had never physically touched a plane,
But often saw them flying across a plain.
Luckily, nobody knew what was happening,
The noise died down or was slackening
Just like when the planes we saw were distancing.

Noise from a subway train and plane was the same.
This was my impression when I first came.
Something new I saw was called a subway,
It was so strange to have a road underway,
People in subway trains to be very okay.
The "Coming to America" movie re-echoed that day.
This was just one of the formal beginnings
I believed there were still many discoveries coming.

I decided to go to the theological seminary
After a long concessionary.
I had been tested with some preliminary,
A preliminary exam, not so ordinary.
America had been in a state so recessionary,
But it was short-lived or temporary.
There, I met scholars of my contemporary,
We often debated on things so unnecessary.

The love of the seminary to some was hereditary,
Who believed thereafter to be legendary.
Some theologians were like a luminary
Who taught the Bible somehow imaginary.
We had a discourse on American racism,
How the system was under heavy criticism.
The church was just a sleeping giant,
A toothless bulldog, puppet, state compliant.

The constitution made churches powerless
In decision-making, they were voiceless.
Government and church had the same fate,
They were all helpless, unable to relate.
We cited many discourses, we had many debates
On how America's fall will be of racism hate.
We cited the Romans with Julian the apostate
Who bragged before every church and every state.

He claimed he needed no God for his empire,
But failed to see his empire would soon expire.
The question was what the church could do
To solve police killings or racism or undo?
Many argued for inter-cultural weddings,
Claiming they would bring down God's blessings
Which would heal our racial hurts hearts.
Its democracy trampled with reckless incapacity.

Inter-racial weddings, it seemed really hard,
I contended such a debate after many hearings.
God created just one man and one race,

Man created many gods and racial race.
We all needed divine love to be united,
A cultural metissage that made us excited.
America was truly racist and divided,
The Ku Klux Klan, I reminded and cited.

That police hate, or KKK all coincided
With white nationalism which it invited.
A cultural metissage was not a racial solution,
Racism in America was seen as an illusion
Where many believed it was out of the equation.
President Obama came in some citation.
If he became the first black president,
It meant the so-called racism was an accident.

Despite police hate, crime, or other incidents
Being the 44th president wasn't a coincidence
But a divine message to make us confident.
Should we define racism just from an incident
Like Trayvon Martin's murder or homicide,
Where he was killed, and justice denied?
Every man has within him red blood.
Why then do some races try to others exterminate?

For me, racism was a real, undeniable reality.
It was so apparent to see open animosity
Between the police and a black community.
Blacks were still the target of racism so unjust.
Think of Emmett Till, killed to rust
For just jesting with a white girl in lust.
Did you forget about Timothy Coggins,
For a white woman's sake, was sent to a coffin?

What of Ed Johnson, wrongly convicted
For sexual assault on a white woman was afflicted.
Was this not a form of racism as depicted?
What about the Scottsboro Boys' false allegation
For raping two white girls in a train in motion?
They were sentenced to life in racial discrimination,

Yet white baboons rape innocent babes daily,
Justice waived in the court rooms as victims black.

FOURTEENTH CANTO
The Writing Of Miss Angel

I was fully assured of today's racism
Which has created a great schism.
Racism in America was like a cobweb,
America's soul was in a deep dark web.
It was evident in the life of many adolescents
Who struggled to live a life of luminescent
To gain love and joy, short-lived or evanescent.
America, I knew, was called a melting pot.

You could be wrongly accused by a plot,
Get convicted, thrown to jail to rust or rot.
As a young man, I aspired to one day get a wife,
But feared my fate, not getting a racist knife.
Some women had become like a wild knife
Who would use the law to kill you alive.
Marriage was a game of fun and for fun,
Broken marriages were the norm for gaming fond.

Relationship trust was of love distrust,
People married for wrong reasons or lust,
America was falling apart with laws unjust.
Money and sex was what many loved or discussed,
Men were reduced to their demise or dust,
By women who lived on child support's intrust.
Most women knew the law, already to thrust,
They seduced men, got pregnant and did adjust
And filed for child support which was a must
To gain men's wealth and make them rust.
Some women cared little, with lust to robust,
Some women's hearts were as hard as a crust,
Virtuous ones were hard to come across -
Many were churchgoers, but refused the cross.
They claimed to be Christ-like to gain some trust,
But men still feared or had much distrust.

Some had textile props on their bust

To look sexy, lure men to fall or entrust
Them with great wealth, a devilish fussed!
Some used pussy power on men trussed.
They would accept nasty pleasure so combust,
Their deeds were strange, queer, and undiscussed.
Weak and frail men fell, and would later suss.
Some women knew all the laws' antitrust.

To make men believe they were thrust of trust,
Everyone was someone's great dread
As China and Russia were America's threat.
Men dreaded some *femmes fatales* or women.
Some women also dreaded us men.
America struggled on social control.
All had gone sour, God was no longer in control
As many blacks were put on the death roll.

This was the collapse of social morale and order
With the introduction of the new world order.
Chaos was everywhere in the atmosphere,
America lived in terror, dread, or fears
As foreign nations threatened its spheres.
Everything was in a state of topsy turvy,
American's military was her pride sturdy,
But now, America was like a ripe banana outside.
But inside, was like a kind of pesticide.

Men had lost their manhood or potency,
Democracy was in decline with cogency.
The nation needed to be saved with urgency,
Nobody knew what to do with accuracy.
Many had scrambled for the presidency,
But America rotated on the same axis
As men brought dishonor to ballot boxes.

Elections were hacked, a clear prophecy,
Every president was the head of the nation
Who brought their own reforms or creation.
Some were loved, hated in a combination.

America was falling from her throne,
They bragged of the military might of drones,
America was lost in a democratic cyclone
As the nation became technophobic.

Every president only depicted the nation,
Its spiritual state, its lost glory or reputation.
A helpless sue happy society in destruction
When team crooks must gather before instruction.
Men became women; women became men
As wickedness through ungodly powers came in.
Decision makers are not executive, they're demons,
A body without eyes or ears with a president.

FIFTEENTH CANTO
The Three Aristotelian Unities

I was a scholar and graduate of The Humanities
Who had fallen in love with the three Aristotelian unities;
The unity of Time, Action, and Place with its ambiguities.
Aristotle's "On the Arts of Poetry" in many universities
Was taught and sometimes thought despite its ambiguities.
It still played a vital role in literary communities.
I didn't agree with these unities or philosophies.
In today's literature, though it gave me opportunities.
To explore many styles across his ambiguities.
I was not studying Aristotle as a critique of crudities,
Rather, concepts in Greek poetics and tragedies.
To craft a modern-day play depicting social realities.

Aeschylus, Sophocles, and Euripides are my admiration
Whose works were worth action in serious attention.
Complete in itself, of amplitude, in an enriched language
With a variety of artistic devices in a tragic action,
Invoking fear, and anxiety about cleansing or purgation,
Stirred my heart to create verse drama for attraction.
I dreaded at one point, was everyone going to be engaged
In reading and understanding verse drama in satisfaction?
I needed a literary vehicle to carry my concepts,
But struggled with the three Aristotelian unities or precepts.
Not that I could not grasp them, but my audience' reaction.

Every tragic hero has a flaw or an imperfection.
It wasn't my priority, but rather their confession.
Their message was a priority and its interaction.
An interaction in the modern world to bring attraction.
I was not trying to be too verbose to create distraction
By following modern day American writers by abstraction.
Horace, in "The Arts of Poetry," on poetry and drama,
Was to solace me, to heal my literary trauma.
True poetry itself, in any genre, demanded some unity,
And the purpose of any poetic unity was harmony,

Calling for a wise choice of subject and good diction
In meters, styles, themes, and characters in appropriation.
Dramatic poetry, however, also needed some serious care
To paint characters, themes, not for readers to despair.
Poetry and drama as two forms of arts must be compared
Or compelled utilizing poetic unity for everyone to share
In the same aesthetic feelings of joy, anxiety, pain, or fear.

I wrote not as an American, but African-American writer.
I wrote not as a regular poet, but a literary fighter.
Who struggled to rebirth a new form of art with a lighter.
Such a rebirth was to either bring bitterness or laugher.
There was room for me to make verse drama better.
I feared more of the critics of a prolific modern writer,
But not the critics of any sole called writer or waiter.
All writers are writers, not all writers write alike
Modern writers seemed to have gone on strike,
Deterring from Greek or classical arts achievement.

Modern writers themselves are in much disagreement
Some write poetry and drama for entertainment
Where style or form wasn't of interest or any engagement.
True drama and poetry was in a state of bereavement.
Reviving verse drama from extinction required uniquement.

American contemporary writers knew Shakespeare,
But couldn't stand to write like him without any fear.
Many writers used modernism in discourse with peers
To create free verse drama, causing true art to disappear.
Some writers wrote drama or poetry as if they were mere
Arts of low reputation, dialogue with no rule to adhere.
Modern drama and poetry had their place, but often unclear
As to how to blend modern with classic to make it sincere.
These were the loopholes; I saw them as unfair and queer.
As a poet and dramatist or simply an African literalist,
A good blend of classical style, not writing as novelist,

Verse drama was to make me a good moralist
To lampoon the American society from immoral guilt.
I wrote with a mindset of duality or modern pluralist
Who could tap into elements of Shakespearean classicism,
To write in local African colors an art of romanticism.
I was aware of context, and style in its mechanism
Importantly, not wanting to be influenced by fanaticism.
I was not writing for arts' sake, but to keep its didacticism
From the pollution of my Pentecostal monasticism.

Coining or reviving verse drama with African images
Gave me a new form of the literary artistic stage
To blend African local colors with modern literature.
In forms such as poetry or drama in similar nature.
African folklore, poetry or drama is rich in its images.
Without this, African literary arts are mere mirages.
American writers knew little of African images or ranges.
Hollywood has long exhausted classic tales for animation.
Films now lack morality for education or sensitization.
Modern Hollywood is more of an art of technology,
Technology, an art expressed in a new methodology.

Hollywood movies need a new creative wind,
The wind of fresh ideas, new stories to win.
Technology is not self-sufficient, for movies
Technology must embrace new African tales
African tales that speak orature, myth, to prevail.
For example, Black Panther caught many attention
Due to its local African local colors, and other usage,
Gratifying the folklore of Wakanda in a dramatic stage.
 Black Adam, Avatar, have the same line of thought.
Its Africaness contributed to a success theme and plot

I am modern myself, but contemporary on stage,
We must not continue to rely on classicism to assuage
Our inability to write true poetry or drama as past sages.
Secondly, I was trying to tell a story that everyone knew.

Racism was destroying the soul of America; it wasn't new.
I could only explore this via African romanticism,
A way to capture my audience's heart in poeticism.
We may deny the Aristotelian unities based on context,
But we can't deny true poetry or drama in a rapid decline.
Hollywood tries to sustain it with film special effects.
The greatest movies in Hollywood come from great texts.
For any text to be great, we must reconsider or even define
Where we have lost our dignity in literary aesthetics.
Or why our dramatic arts are tasteless, even in poetics.
African literature is the mother of all literature,
It has the fecundity to procreate art in a creative nature.

Let's gain insight into African literature if we are unsure.
African literature has the charms and power to allure,
Richly built-in local metaphors so unique and pure.
African literature is a gamut of written and oral traditions
In Afro-Asiatic languages, with western compositions.
There are both written and oral in scope or expositions.
Written is bound to a small geographic minority,
Oral folklore shares values with the sub-Saharan majority.
Influenced from cultures from the Mediterranean stylistics.
Such as literature by both Hausa and scholars of Arabic.
We can talk about Nigeria; we know of Chinua Achebe
One of the sages, African novelists, poets, and critics.
African literature embraces works of other Amharic
Compositions with its rich Christian traditions of mystics.
African literature in English is just a recent tradition,
Dating back to the 20th century and up for its recognition.

English Language is a pipe for African literary rendition.
It doesn't make African literature an English tradition.
English and African literature are only alike in linguistics,
Not in terms of images alike and characteristics.
Literature of all genres can brag of its oral storytelling,
But oral tradition is an African pride so compelling.
Africans have mythical tales to tell in their dwelling

Using oral composition, performance, and transmission,
Absorbing every audience or member in the elocution.

African literature explores its text from its context
Using inanimate objects to create realism or pretext,
To illustrate the past in a mysterious inaccessible way
Thus elevating its ancestors, in oral narration or play.
African literature speaks variety, it taps from history
To praise its ancestors not exposing their flaws or misery.
Not all storytelling is African in nature or even in orature.
It has distinctive features that make it unique or mature.
Its images, body language, voice articulation or oration
Contributes to most of its successful African tradition.

To be a griot requires one to be a sage to be effective
To understand cultural folklore to be creative.
To capture the past, present and future in a way additive.
In a juxtaposition style that keeps its audience meditative.
Nothing makes African literature addictive as its riddles.

Problems are raised in riddles or in idioms and parables.
Requiring one to think of a solution, till one is wrinkled.
To search through one's intellectual reservoir of fables.
African riddles are logical, not part of its oral poetics.
It calls for a deep inquiry of the audience's heroics.
A figurative but vigorous contrast of reality and fantasy,
Whose metaphorical compositions also create a phantasy.
African literature also shares a rich tradition with its lyrics
Blending the metaphorical, poetic, and dynamic.

Proverbs, an African source of palm oil eaten with words,
Is the libation of sages who contextually speak forward.
African literature is unique, heroic poetry, panegyric
Praising its ancestors in its traditional tales or epic.

SIXTEENTH CANTO
Racism in American School Systems

Many years of struggles in New York went by,
Some of my pains and fears I could boldly say goodbye.
It was clear on my mind; I was to focus on verse comedy,
To use words to create special effects in dramatic melody.
I could play with many styles including word monody.
A hungry man is an angry man, as often said in an adage.
I was fast maturing physically and growing of age,
The need for financial independence came to me with rage

With much pressure to get a high paying profession.
I was trained in literary studies, which I loved with passion,
But this alone I couldn't rely on to put food on my table,
Most jobs in The Humanities were very scarce or low-paid,
And required a terminal degree or to have been well-read.
I had finished my seminary studies, with some dread,
What and where to go next, fear did my heart shred.
I studied what I loved; I was happy, no financial relief.

My landlord cared not about what I knew or believed
When it came to collecting rent every four weeks.
I had to figure out other best means or techniques
To earn a living, not just by drama, or reading theology.
I struggled with the vicious capitalist circle and ideology.
It was many months at post-graduation to earn a living.
I needed something new, financially better or enriching.
I finally enrolled again in school to study cybersecurity,
I applied myself to leaning it with much sincerity.

Yes, I needed something better, a financial prosperity,
Capitalism was similar to slavery in its rationality.
It created slaves by providing promises, whereas in priority
They needed their labor to make their gain on the minority.
American schools operated with a capitalist mentality,
Educational philosophies sought to hide this reality.
I joined a community college; new with immaturity,

To the system, which I later found with much obscurity.

They had a system in place that truly lacked maturity.
This system was of ages longer with capitalist popularity.
Students were to take forcefully ESL college classes,
Especially if you were black or from other race classes.
English as a Second Language was for non-English speakers.
The good news was that you came to school with sneakers,
Nobody cared provided you paid the money they needed,

Then, they cared not whether you failed or succeeded.
They had a series of junk courses to follow, not needed.
This made me sick and almost gave up defeated.
Nobody cared about anything, everyone was treated
With capitalist interest, with much pride that exceeded
That exhibited their human ego of western superiority
On non-American English speakers or African minority.

With a bachelor's degree in English and literature,
I was still required to evaluate for them to make sure
I could speak English, American English, of course,
Since everything not American was of no-good course.
This was an insult to African educational institutions,
To take ESL with a bachelor's degree as the solution
For college enrollment to further my education.
I spoke English so well without any pollution.
I spoke the English language, not by evolution.

We were taught English as a means of communication.
British Received Pronunciation was a form substitution.
The Queen's language came to Africa by revolution.
 My accent seemed worthless to any academic contribution.
To capitalist education system, a system called execution
Used to extort money or make gain known as tuition.
I started school in full guilt, wishing for absolution.
I wasn't a criminal, but need some consolation.
I took my first English lessons with some circumlocution.

It was intentional to draw the teacher's attention.
That capitalist education held me in a detention.
I excelled in my two classes worth great admiration.
This began to make some sense or even drew attention.
I thought out-performing was to give me some exemption
Or gain some form of preferential treatment in conclusion,
But I erred in my judgment, and perhaps anticipation.
I went to the department head of English ESL education,

With much hope and assurance of good communication,
I was too qualified for that class to be in confusion.
I got into her office; she smiled with mixed affection.
Was her mixed affection going to give me satisfaction?
I was also greatly concerned about her direction.
We spoke for a while just as I had in my projection.
She refused to allow me into my major—cybersecurity.
I needed two years of ESL classes to gain perfection.
Many were in the same system in their majority.

English Language, a common core course or intersection
They believed it worked for many students' futurity.
Was it worth wasting my precious time on this rejection?
I spent days and even weeks in deep reflection.
I went to school one day for our English examination.
I had a friend in school I was in good relation.
Some teachers also understood my worries and objections.
They were black teachers; some had similar recollections,

They were not happy, but dreaded to incite insurrection.
My main English teacher traveled to another nation.
We had a substitute teacher to give our final examination.
She was racist, she ruined my day in damnation.
When she began to grade my English composition.
When the exam began, she was in circumspection.
She went around our desks, furious, doing some inspection.

Her presence gave nothing but an intellectual contusion.

The exam was two hours after which we will get a grade
In one hour, I finished the exam went to her in a parade.
I walked to her, and she thought I needed help or some aid,
But I turned in my paper and she nodded in disapproval,
Yelled with harsh and brutal racial elocution hard to evade.
No student had ever beaten this record in half an hour.
She took my paper, wore her goggles for a deeper perusal.
Then, she shook her head in what meant refusal
To admit that I had everything right in just half an hour!

She sat on a chair as a wooden carved masquerade.
She flipped my paper over attempting to degrade.
She looked much alike with Chaucer's wife of Bath,
Like a destitute woman who has never taken a bath.
Her lipstick was as dark as rain beaten charcoal
She was neither a young woman nor even old.
She was just a terrible creature I couldn't describe
Though she claimed to have a Ph.D. as a scribe.
She looked like a photocopied letter of Willie Lynch.

I hated everything about her, I meant every inch.
Her butts were fat like water in an inflated balloon
With eyes and ears like that of a civilized baboon.
Her waist was as tiny and small as that of a wasp.
A chronic racist, an asthmatic patient who did gasp.
She wore a wig which was as ugly as the hair of a pig
Her mouth odor was like rotten egg when she did speak.
I am not sure she was a woman; she was just anyhow.
She looked like a doll or puppet with no eyebrow.

She bragged to be the doyen of creative arts and English.
How could she be when she was just dumb and foolish?
How could she be when she had not written any book?
She was a pseudo intellectual, an academic crook.
Even the powder on her face was like particles of dust

Which she used a duster to dust the previous dusk.
Her dental structure was like a camel's toe
That was why her high heels she wore were all faux.

I was so offended with her racial facial expressions,
But was ready to challenge her with great affirmation.
She called my English teacher and complained,
Hoping to get any evidence to have me restrained.
She was shocked; she found nothing negative or obtained.
When she learnt my IQ was above the ESL to contain.
She came and apologized with mixed feelings of shame.
Racism in the American school system became certain.
I left the school that day with thoughts so uncertain.

I had plans to foster my education despite this humiliation.
I spent the night searching for schools and information
That offered my desired studies or concentration.
I decided to do distance education to avoid any relation
That was to breed other racial forms of confrontation.
I had a bachelor, I finally concluded in my observation
To get a master's degree, but I was asked an evaluation.

I waited for weeks to get an evaluation completion.
It came alas! I applied to another school for admission.
I waited for their response for acceptance indication,
But doubted if I could cope with a master's degree.
I was even confused the more even ready to disagree
Why they thought I could not complete this degree.
They knew my degree was from Cameroon University
So, it was not up to the American standard in diversity.

Another opened discrimination and racism?
I lashed out with verbal opposition and criticism.
I asked them to explain why they thought they knew it all,
Or if the American educational system had no flaw.
They finally asked me to write an essay or dissertation
Which was what I loved best to disproof their notion

That Africans are low in IQ or had poor institutions.
Racism to some Americans was like superstition
Your nationality classified your identification.

I spent the night reading my dictionary to be eloquent
To write a dissertation flawless in theme development.
What the heck they thought of my underdevelopment
They wanted to discredit my degree or grandiloquence!
A racist educational system that resounded with resonance
In my ears when I was writing, spelling out consonance
Just to make sure I proved them wrong with evidence.

I wrote my essay with a high tone and diction.
I didn't fear getting from them any contradiction.
American education was full of verbosity or decadence.
They insulted my education or had no reference.
Anything that wasn't American, had no excellence.
A pseudo-education devoid of standard intelligence!
I didn't care with my word usage or deference
Since I knew they were racists without benevolence.

Now, let's be realistic and compare both institutions.
I was finally admitted, and I discovered this involution.
The so-called standard education was an under-education
Aimed at converting my brain to a diluted education.
Africa was advanced in its educational curriculum
Where I spent years reading books in their volumes.
Some American curriculum in school ached my reticulum,
But I feared more damages on my diverticulum.
The whole system was ludicrous and very ridiculous

After thinking I was going in for something meticulous.
Such under-education wasn't worth a scholarly stimulus,
It could retard one's intellect to a speed of a limulus.
I was disappointed, I couldn't see any real impetus
That could stimulate my intellectual appetite or apparatus.
The education's ecosystem suffered was so ambiguous,

It lacked clarity, scope or content deemed unambiguous.
It was most approximately competing with Corona virus,
A dangerous indoctrination similar to a colonial virus
Introduced in African to corrupt the elite righteous.
My passion soon declined to a state less desirous.

Of course, there was nothing new to learn or to inspire us.
The system made one to be a robot of ideology
With a grading system of 4.0 GPA or numerology;
A false measurement of students' IQ - ology.
I even thought their grading system came from astrology
Which gave false glittering hopes like stars in heaven.
Though many teachers made of it a financial haven.

The scholastic systems only gave a form of knowledge,
Some of this knowledge so useless to one's stoppage.
Richest and successful people never finished college.
Why waste money on a pseudo-educational blockage?
Institutions had big endorsements just for a homage.
A pseudo-education to keep one in moral bondage.

I could learn much from Bill Gates and other sages,
Ralph Lauren and Steve Jobs, though of different ages,
Mark Zuckerberg and James Cameron much engaged
To educate the youths on how to earn great wages.
With all this, we were called shithole in an old adage,
A stylistic device ***ad hominem*** against us, we, all blacks.

SEVENTEENTH CANTO
America Repent

"America, 'Mene, Mene, Tekel.
Perverse and adulterous generation,
You have made racism your habitation.
Your dwelling is now an abomination.
Like a kissing bug, you drink innocent blood,
You are tainted with blood, your name is in mud,
And your pride is in your supremacy and diplomacy.
My children are weeping for your mercy."

"You call them black, shithole unmerited,
You spill their blood with such a high-spirited,
Racial brutality, so brutally unlimited.
How long in the pride of your abomination
Shall you provoke my fist to rise for justice?
Oh America! America! America!
Instead of crying for my grace and mercy,
You want to be great again through diplomacy."

"Out of my womb, I conceived your impurity,
From British wars, I kept you to maturity.
Your belly is prideful, but you are very okay.
From your mouth stinks bills of decay,
For you think you know it all or the way.
Truly you are blind; you have fallen astray,
And from your mouth stinks bills of decay
As you threw God out in your democracy."

"Oh America! America! America!
I had set you on a worldwide throne this high
A throne of honor that no currency can buy.
I gave you wings, taught you to fly,
You learnt to fly, but now want to fly wild.
You dishonor me, and my name you defile.
You now sound the trumpet of a vain battle cry
With injustice in your streets that my eyes decry."

"I hate some of your ways!

Amend some of your ways!
I am the Alpha and the Omega,
The Beginning and the End
In whose hand America was birthed,
In whose hand America can be crushed.
America, I birthed you, I gave your breath,
You drank water from my palms as it gushed."

Oh America! America! America!
Be still and know I am your God,
From and through the Delaware River,
I walked your forefathers across without a quiver.
They sang of joy of victory; I gave them quicker.
As Moses crossing the Red Sea to Canaan,
So was George Washington to a new homeland,
A New Canaan, a new homeland called America.

"You were slaves and refugees in a strange land,
I saw the cruelty of your Egypt in England,
You were a virgin without breast nor garland,
I guided you across rivers with my hand,
I made you a City Upon the Hill, a dreamland,
A dreamland of freedom, liberty, and equality,
But you have fallen in the same condemnation;
The damnation caste of racial inequality."

"Oh America! America! America!
Have you forgotten that love so soon
Which was in your old and odd days a cocoon?
Did I not save you from the cruelty of the typhoon?
Why are your elites calling themselves tycoons
Bragging to have been born with a silver spoon
While their hands are filthy with blood;
The blood of those who matter to me?"

"Oh America! City Upon the Hill!
Be still and know, **I Am Who I Am!**
The **I Am** of Washington, your forefathers.
If you believed in the dream of your forefathers

Whom I led as a stray child without a mother,
Why can't you love "the negro" as your brother?
Why can't you listen to my instruction
Or take to heart my rebuke and correction?"

"Didn't your forefathers obey in the storm?
Am I not old enough to teach you wisdom?
In my wisdom,
I mapped the heavens and the earth,
The world has seen my glory and wonders.
Have you ever seen my ways go blunder?
Have my thoughts or promises ever wandered?
Your wisdom is vain and nothing to ponder."

"You bear my name on your bills in vain,
This to achieve your manipulative evil gain.
I have waited for you to repent for so long,
But in your pride, you see no wrong
In the affliction of my people bleeding
Whose blood in your streets are pleading.
The new world order have you embraced
To defile my name, and now you stand braced."

"America, Mene, Mene, Tekel.
You are busy conducting same-sex marriages,
Bragging and claiming to do my will,
But I have given you all the free will
To be free, but you've been caged in cages.
My wrath boils against you in full rage.
Only for my remnant's tears of supplication
Have I refrained and I've been tolerant."

"Tolerant for the cross' sake and blood covenant
Shed by my son, Jesus for America on the cross,
And in your remnant's vein, it flows across.
I am not the God of the New World Order.
Novos Ordos Seclorum—
You seduced my elites in that speech disorder
With rotten bills by men with mental disorder.

Consider your ways and come back to me again,
Consider your ways to be made great again."

"America, Mene, Mene, Tekel.
Consider your ways to be born again.
Then I may prosper you like a fig tree,
And I will bring your foes to their knee.
The cup of your abomination is full,
You are now standing like a hornless bull.
Your hands are soiled by counts of blood
Do you remember these bloodsheds?"

"The Battle of Tippecanoe-1811?
The First Seminole War (1816-1818)?
The Indian Removal Act (1830)?
The Black Hawk War (1832)?
The Sand Creek Massacre (1864)?
The Red Cloud's War (1866)?
The Battle of the Little Bighorn (1876)?
The blood of generations is in your hands."

"America, Mene, Mene, Tekel.
Repent, else, I will make you a global fool.
Return to me; I will clothe you with a virgin wool.
Your breast will be nation's delight,
They shall bask in your democratic sun-light.
How do you want me to defend you
When your deeds are abominable in my sight?
Your racial sins and crimes are ugly in my sight."

I am the Lord of Hosts, master of warfare.
Return, I will restore your welfare.
Remember the height you've fallen.
Return to me before my wrath is befallen.
My scroll of judgment is now opened
Revelation 6:1-17. Peace! Peace! Peace!

I AM THE I AM
I WILL BE WHO I WILL BE
I WILL BE WHAT I WILL BE

EIGHTEENTH CANTO
The Church In America

My judgment alone might be unfair
Of scenes or sins seen to breed despair.
Like Chaucer's Canterbury Tales of saints,
I had seen the same doctrine with evil restraints.
Let's perhaps talk it through Miss. Beatrice's discourse,
Of this unholy, perverse religious intercourse.
It is still part of my story, autobiography, of course.
Miss Beatrice had once upon a time a boyfriend.

Her boyfriend of a megachurch were Pastor Judge,
She was vexed by him; then she kept him a grudge.
Pastor Judge preached with holiness and divine fire,
But he was like a lecherous dog consumed by fire.
He could not see any budussy stand or even come by.
This little guy would make his alleluia to be high.
He would change his sermon's tone for poontang pie.
I knew he was possessed by and for a pussycat.

And his best meal after preaching was a pussyrat.
Of course, pussycat or pussyrat with a black hat.
He was libido sexcess, or sexist of so excessive,
A unique man, very rare, obsessive, and aggressive.
One mourning morning, he found his demise
In a harlot's house, in her, or by her budussy.
He might have died of ecstasy or pussy stroke,
Even at sixty-nine, he was a man very handsome.

He was very hot, sassy, obsessed with sixty-nine.
He was a virtuous pastor, a free and generous giver,
He had a good taste for everything, and loved eating beaver.
Then he praised God in tongues every morningasm.
He preached against sin often, with much sarcasm,
But himself loved eating the breakfast-of-champions.
He was a scholar of the "morning constitution,"
He craved for "morning treatment" than the Bible.

He was all in one, a gifted chef always able
To please his church, even cooking pancakes
To please them since they also loved seggs.
She loved God, but he "made her love come down!"
He had an "o-spot" car, always parked downtown.
He preached like thunder, sometimes would scream.
When he felt too much anointing, he would cream.
Nothing could stop him from going all the way.

He also had a good mussy and loved prophecy,
The spirit of his prophecy would overpower you.
To praise him like a choirmaster in egasm.
He went from house to house, all his way
To cast devils and demons of all mouthgasm.
Once delivered, he praised God after glow.
He even won the best demon chaser Oscar
As he was named "twilight" superstar.

He was sometimes mistaken for a dentist,
His teeth were all aligned like a camel's toe.
He also claimed he was also a gospel artist.
His best praise song was "jizzy woo woo,"
Where he spent all the tithes and offerings.
That's when you saw his teeth, brown and old.
I will let you all judge by their own fruits,
A tree with very bad fruits might mean bad roots.

My hurts were more in the church than outside,
I was bitten and beaten by a religious reptile
A false gospel of prosperity, very far or wide.
There were other strings, other things done wild
To entice men and women to come and confide
And would be prayed for and preyed on later on,
I saw much evil in the church; it went on and on.
I was compelled to speak as part of the body.

The church was contrary to what it oathed to embody.
They prayed day and night for hours till soppy.

Many preached well but lived a sinful hobby.
Let me tell you the story of somebody, a believer.
He was the most righteous and perfect ever,
A perfect gentleman and follower of Christ,
So devout to his self-piety to be evil-enticed,
A man to have in your or every congregation.

Permit me to introduce him to you all, James.
I am sure he was named after Saint James.
It's not proper to suggest or call people names,
You would soon discover during these Olympic games
The truth about church messianic confession claims.
Whatever a man sowed, so he did reap be it like.
He claimed to be divine or knew Christ's dislike.
He proclaimed heavenward desires, dreams-like.
But mocked others without food or on hunger strike.

He had abundance, just as every Pharisee,
He bragged about being the best Christian or Sadducee,
There is an end to our pilgrimage here on earth.
We shall stand the great Armageddon of rebirth,
And give an account of our lives to Elohim.
It shall be at His discretion to judge him.
God is the righteous Judge and shall judge all.

A gentleman, a church verb, proverb, or a synonym
Who could accept anything such as a pseudonym
To meet his needs. What a disgrace to the gospel hymn
Which he sang every day as an angel of light!
Tasteless salt of the earth void of its delight.
Don't get distracted and miss your flight,
Everyone has an individual heavenward flight.
Life is a battle; we must aim to righteously fight.

Access not every access even at a green light.
Greenlight to some access requires insight.
Insight to access a green light requires foresight.
Foresight to assess or access any green light despite
All the pleasures it might bring or lure us into.

I have much to say; there is "Much Ado About Nothing,"
Right confession and repentance comes like morning dew.
I am confused and fused without further ado, adieu!

NINETEENTH CANTO
Miss Angel: Fiction of Reality?

My soul or spirit was perturbed and troubled,
The laws were enacted, by it many stumbled.
What was meant for a common good became sin,
Nobody cared, everybody dared, nor had ever seen
The apocalypse of hell, dreadful and horrible scene
Awaiting America for her abominable fate soobscene.
No race was safer to find love, get a wife or marry,
The law made every race litigious foes of merry.

It was hard to define one's fate, faith, fade, or state.
911— most *femmes fatales* were specialized specialists.
Like Asunder, some were evil pregnant perfectionists.
African women were tamed by the game so fast,
They were so evil in mind or in line to contrast.
When some women became a registered nurse,
Her or their jobless husband became a curse.
She or they would tongue-lash him so perverse.

That he would regret or bemoan why he got married.
Men became slaves, enslaved slaves so varied,
Some baby-seated or falsely accused of rape.
They were wedged so hard not to escape.
Men ended up killing or smothering their wives.
Most often, either they used guns or knives.
Some *femmes fatales* with money and sex,
Devoured men mercilessly like a t-rex.

They had 911 for them or always by their side
To defend them at any time with feminist pride.
All races seemed racists, not safer at any cost,
They seemed to have the same agenda or course.
Marrying in one's culture, Afro-culture was surest,
Africa still remained our final home of and for rest
Where Afro-culturalists retire without police arrest.
Who was the best woman I was to ever marry?

I dreaded them all, Miss Asunder like Mary
For the planted missiles on the stage to marry.
Miss Angel was my better half or perfect match
As we met and fell in love sometime in March.
Miss Angel is nothing but a true and fictional
Embodiment of that long-yearned love unconditional.
Everyone desired love, be loved so unrestricted,
But many ended up by the law's jaw hurt or afflicted.

Love and marriage were a contentious bed of roses,
They either caused joy or pains called hypnosis.
Getting married required a good divine prognosis.
I understood this immensely in my analysis
That marriage and love were known as osmosis
Where a stronger solution pulls a weaker solution.
The poem "A Bed of Roses" was the evolution
Of my dilemma, anxieties that formed a revolution.

This would later be my anchor for divine inspiration
Despite all, marriage was a divine institution.
My parents' love affair flashed back in consolation.
I needed a stronger reason to marry or resolution,
I had thought love/marriage were beds of roses.
I saw many of such beds of roses without roses.
I asked myself, "When shall the roses genuinely grow
When all love seekers lived in anguish and sorrow?

If today's marriage was bleak, what of tomorrow?
Love and marriage were a sort of item in borrow.
Everyone looked for a perfect love or virtuous hero,
But feared the sacrificial path so painfully narrow.
Celebrity tales or marriages were all vanity in life.
Though I still needed to get a real uncelebrity wife,
I thought of few real celebrities who lived as pair,
A one-time *Romeo and Juliet* now in despair.

In a sue happy society, everyone feared,
They feared the love deception that often appeared.
They feared that their money could disappear,

They feared love was a sham, nobody cared,
They feared many things unknown or unclear,
They feared the society had become so weird.
They feared many broken hearts seen or heard,
They feared broken hearts needed to be reared.

They feared lawsuits for rape were on the gear.
They feared materialism made love cheered,
They feared fame enticed love or lured it revered.
They feared when one fell in love or volunteered.
They feared famous intermarriages with peered.
They feared to marry but prenuptial or adhered.
They feared love was lust-motivated or engineered.
They feared the law was merciless and interfered.

They feared their past woes could reappear.
They feared the evil behind the law could pioneer.
They feared people's hearts were evilly steered.
They feared that their reputation could be smeared.
They feared not to be love-enticed but sneered.
They feared love could any time change or veer.
They feared that love enticed lawsuits persevered.
They feared not to have their hearts again sheared.

They feared the media's gossip, aired to be eared.
They feared anything that glittered or endeared.
They feared fake butts or breasts to their hearts seared
They feared friends' satire, irony or not be jeered
They feared their love cracks would be premiered.
They feared their wealth in divorce commandeered.
They feared their hearts shouldn't be fiercely speared.
They feared divorce aftermath anguished leered.

Many lived their lives on others, or others dared.
Romeo was never truly insane or wrong
To die by Juliet when he thought she was gone.
An exemplary love tale of such, many longed.
Things had fallen apart, materialism so strong,
Lured men and women to sing a love song

To entice each other in an illusion life-prolong,
For no one wants love that will not last long.

If marriage was truly a bed of virtuous roses,
In a sue-happy society, love never had roses.
If I fell in love and truly found one tomorrow,
Was nemesis going to bring me joy or sorrow?
Life was unfair, love or marriage unpredictable.
Once beaten or bitten with woes unforgettable,
Your life ended up miserable or deplorable.
Such thoughts made me already uncomfortable.

Poetry and drama were my catharses of trust.
They assured me of a life of trust without rust,
A spontaneous recollection of feelings was just
For me to write down my distrust in disgust.
Like Romeo thought Juliet was rusting,
On the contrary, she was just in her state resting.
Both lovers ended up resting and rusting
As both were at forth sight still lusting.

If I forsook poetry and drama for a wife,
I dreaded nothing more than Romeo's fate in life.
However, I still needed an Afro-cultural wife
If I needed to be a man or remain complete.
Love or marriage wasn't a race to compete,
But a decision for life, a decision to commit
That every contamination my eyes saw delete
For a true and motherly love we commit.

Knowing that Miss Asunder could come in,
Come in at any time, by the law,
Through the law to put asunder true love
To look for any means, by the law or flaw,
Take nothing of her dangerous favors flow
As is the greatest trap of American looting women;
To trap your life's love or marriage a mirage,
"Lord," I implored, "help me to get engaged."

TWENTIETH CANTO
Miss Asunder And Miss Beatrice

Miss Asunder, a white race supremacist,
Ended up or finally earned a sad nemesis.
There is one law, that law is called love,
It's above everything; it comes from above.
As a poet and skillful autobiographer,
I decided not to speak as a biographer.
Not to reduce the story potency just for admiration,
But to keep a flow of the reader's attention.

I am a man with a free heart and love for all races,
I wrote with a writer's voice, not racist.
I wrote to correct, rebuke racists that did exist,
I wrote to comfort the people's heart or assist.
Permit me to introduce you my character,
Of my favorite, let's begin with Miss Asunder.
None existed as Asunder, don't be alarmed in wonder,
For there are many asunder on everyone's destiny's ladder.

As an artist, biographer, poet, and creative writer,
She was, she is, and she will always be
In her late thirties, a native of American aborn.
A Caucasian of color, not colored, very pretty adorn!
A fairly tall, curved, and curvy heavy hips,
Well-polished hips as appealing as heart-shaped lips.
With long brown hair lashing her backside,
Her beauty and vanity are more than a touristic site.

When she walks on heels, she provokes asides
From onlookers, men especially with foresight
Who understand the true haste and taste of beauty.
In a world of beauty contest full of bounty and bootie,
She's a woman of modest goggles who gargles
And thinks she's so smart because she uses Google
With extravagant classical mannerism and bangles
As the beauty of her long earrings dangle.

She is a woman of great wealth and great health,
Others call her President of the Commonwealth!
She is not only healthily wealthy but ostentatious,
But ostentatiously wealthy and healthy in pride.
Her fame in the city is contagious and contentious,
She's pseudo-shrewd, pretentious, and capricious.
She's innocently innocent, dangerous of a bride
For any man who falls into her trap in misguide!

There are many others of her prototype or type
Who dress flashily or flamboyantly in miniskirts
With long fingernails like beggars in the outskirts
Who think beauty and sex open every door,
But frail and fail to know that beauty void of character
Is madness, mundanity, vanity, or mere folklore
That fades all of a sudden like a beauty décor,
For deep painting makes a beautiful woman art.

She lives in a vast mansion in New York City,
A mansion as vast as the city's capital.
Lights from her mansion from afar
Glitter with high immensity and propensity
Like disco lights from all nightclubs in the city.
Despite her grandeur, she can settle for anything less,
She isn't careless, but she cares less unless
She gets what she wants anyhow less!

Here is she entrapped in her unhappy loneliness
So desperately stressed, lonely and loveless,
Watching Hollywood's Romeo and Juliet.
Of the time fast past, she regrets,
Wishing to have been or be in Juliet's shoe
To have a man she can love and glue too;
A man like Romeo, who can stand on the balcony
And beg for her love in truth and even in agony.

Now lost in her thought in despair and cacophony,
Then thinks she of Tchinda, the elegant poet,
A poet of ambiance who might love some moet,

But he just arrived from Cameroon, March 03, 2010.
Enter Miss Beatrice with much zeal and eagerness,
Her face speaks brightly of hope and merriness.
But what could be that her face lightens up?
She's alike beautiful, but of tanned skin color.

She mixes all colors on her face for makeup.
She's Africanly aborned, adorned with no mistake,
She's naturally pretty with well-admired breast
Supported with textile props to stand at rest!
She's now Americanized in her English accent,
She sometimes speaks English with words so archaic.
She brags of her African decent culture and descent,
Her high heels are as tall as the Empire State Building.

New York City has earned her the name sexy baby,
Perhaps that's why her favorite song is a lullaby.
She only smiles when she's on heat or money needs
That make her gentle and polite to hide her misdeeds.
Her eyes can move up and down like a doll.
When she lashes or snubs at you, that's all.
You never think of talking to her again;
Only bourgeois who are willing for a good bargain.

The big guys in the city come with big cars,
Some come with big baggies, not her class.
It is obvious she's expensive but a lady of class
Looking for men with a name or destiny to devour.
Her smile is a blend never understood by victims
Whether African or American as they are classy.
Big catches make her regain a concealed smile, a metaphor;
A Cameroonian more American than Americans!

TWENTY-FIRST CANTO
A Sue-Happy Society

What is a sue-happy society?
Let's look it up without anxiety.
Merriam-Weber dictionary defines it for us,
"disputatious, contentious, in a litigious mood."
Prone to engage in lawsuits, watch out dude!
Watch out the way you drink or eat even food.
What is really a sue-happy society?
You can eat and get sued by your own stomach.

What again is a sue-happy society?
If your stomach is black and food white, you're finished.
If you go to the courtroom, you won't come back.
Live like a saint, without spot, wrinkle, or blemish.
When you eat and bite your tongue by accident,
Your tongue will make it litigious or an incident.
You will be sued, tried, and forced to accept your guilt.
If you plead not guilty, you will face the wrath of the hilt.

If you're back, they will give you huge fines,
They will give you on their deadlines.
What is a sue-happy society?
When a snake bites you, it is its right.
If you bite it back by day or by night,
Its lawyers will sue you and try you as a criminal,
You will be sentenced for eternity, no minimal,
For a cursed snake has more rights than a human.

What is a sue-happy society?
When you are wealthy like a celebrity,
They hate you and seek your downfall or integrity.
They will testify against you in court with audacity,
You will be accused of rape in the dream or city.
Even flies without wings or full or vulgarity
Will say you groped them with hands of density
An interesting court mapping down celebrities.

What is a sue-happy society?

When you breath without others' permission,
You are sued, sued without a proper definition.
You will be tried, as often, made culpable.
There are laws for everything immutable,
Laws to make you guilty and inevitable.
When you get choked by your own saliva,
Your tongue or teeth will sue you forever.

What is a sue-happy society?
They call it a constitutional right whenever.
They are above the law; they are always clever.
They make all the laws and control them, however.
They implement the laws against whoever,
They hate black, ugly, dirty or whatever.
If you are black and stand for your rights,
They will pass a law, anti-rioter's rights.

What is a sue-happy society?
That interesting movement empowers
Laws to devalue your rights or seek to override
Your right to freedom, protest against a brutish police
Who will happily kneel on your neck as they please!
If your color is not black, it's okay by the law,
But if your color is black as police, its treason
For even your smile is criminally culpable.

What is a sue-happy society?
If you look at yourself in the mirror and smile,
Just be patient awhile.
They will bang your door with force so hostile.
Your mirror will then file a lawsuit against you,
They will make you guilty and helpless to undo.
If you look like someone else in resemblance,
And that person you look like is a white in semblance.

What is a sue-happy society?
When your eyes see a woman by mistake,
If you are rich, then your wealth is at stake,
She will say you raped her with your sight,

113

She will demand reparation or jailed inside.
If you are black, they will sue you for millions.
Since you are black, you have no opinions
If you are black, they file a lawsuit for intimidation.

What is a sue-happy society?
A society of lawyers and disroyal.
If you can't trust a policeman, so are lawyers.
When they see money, they can be very loyal.
When they see money, they can tell the judge in court,
A giraffe is a type of money, they have evidence to support.
This the pandemic of a sue happy society.
Live and let's live with mixed anxiety.

TWENTY-SECOND CANTO
Book Revelation And Struggles

I sometimes wrote by inspiration
In Harlem, New York, it was by revelation.
Every good gift comes from above,
Not from abroad, but from true divine love.
Miss Angel was first a romantic poem of love.
It later became a religious play or drama,
Then finally, I made it a political drama,
For the verses were blowing my mind.

It had different versions or editions
Written under different harsh conditions.
In my dreams, I was visited by messengers,
They were angels, not just passengers.
They came with a blank paper or scroll,
My spiritual being was enlightened as a whole.
When I woke up in the blessed dawn,
I went to a retreat or became withdrawn.

Then, inspiration will begin to flow.
It flowed and flooded me with an overflow.
I wrote in seasons when heaven's gates
Were opened, my soul did steadfast await.
There were seasons when heavens did speak,
Inspiration by revelation came to me in a heap.
Some were enlightening; my spirit did leap,
Leap with great joy, verses robbing me of sleep.

My creative intuitions were awake and did creep.
I wrote artfully and tactfully, sometimes in weeps,
Some of what I saw on my mind's imagination or peeps,
Peeps of heavenly things, as to my heart's sweeps.
My thoughts were fierce and as strong as a jeep
As heaven did reveal them to me in seeps.
I was just privileged of such relations to reap
That knocked at my conscience with a beep.

I wrote like one climbing on a mountain's steep
In conditions unpleasant to my finger's tip,
Some were apocalyptic, worthy of just a peek
To see today's reality, racism so bleak.
I was dexterous in the art of poetry technique
To coin my thoughts in verse drama so unique.
Sometimes, a dream woke me up with a creak.
This sometimes occurred in days or a week.

Heaven was always ready to reveal or speak
As much as I gave my heart to it or did seek,
Heaven spoke in parts that came like a leak.
Precept after precept, I saw and did predict.
It's hard to tell all I saw or truly heard as a squeak,
I saw one angelic being, heavily built in physique,
An angel of war, perhaps, dreadful but meek,
And the angel of good news for solution weeks.

Certainly, he could be, and was the prince of peace
Who visited me for more grease and also increase;
An increase of knowledge that never will decrease.
I wrote many books, about five in 2010 or a year.
What was from above gave boldness over my fear.
The prince of darkness came against me so fierce
With sore affliction, so fierce that it did pierce
My desire to aspire to write so well as Shakespeare.

At one point, I was deterred by something unclear.
Hunger and loneliness in New York City did appear,
Reminding me that a hungry man is an angry man
That was when my woes and worries also began.
I was still weak in New York City, a seminarian,
Who had aspired to be a genuine theologian.
I struggled with poetry and hunger to remain utopian
I had few friends, Africans, some Ethiopian.

We were all seminarians with a lot of variants.
We had different backgrounds, others Smithsonian.

Some theologians called themselves Newtonian
Just as I was one, but also called myself poetician,
But not politician.
After weeks of hunger and anger, I got a job
After I had gone through the ailment of Job.
I was a dishwasher in a small restaurant,
It made me very happy to see dollars as a debutant.

I lived in Harlem, worked in Manhattan, downtown,
I learnt to eat American cuisine as a clown.
As an employee, we had free meals during break,
During break, I ate much, fast, unseen, or opaque.
I ate all that was on the cuisine's menu, such as cakes.
I not only ate when hungry, I also ate for hunger's sake.
I ate, drank soda, and made sure I made no mistake.
I struggled with sleep at work, but fought to stay awake.

At the end of the day, I went back home very late,
I felt good; my belly was full and in a good state.
I loved the restaurant because the food was great,
But it made me gain a lot of weight.
The restaurant paid us a very low, minimal rate.
Well, it meant little to me, I was glad not to debate,
I just needed my belly full and to be up to date
Such that when hungry, I could think and write.

I later quitted; I found a job with Macy,' a retailer.
After being hired, a night before, I feared failure,
I was to work ringing up customers or a cashier.
We had too many rules and dressing codes to adhere.
I had my greatest nightmare, or rather my fear.
What was the difference between a dime and a penny?
I died many times before I got to work that noon,
All I knew was that it was a currency or money.

Only mathematics was to deliver me from my doom,
But when at night I was out strong to see the moon
Whose quietness often erased the sad day esteem,
I now thought of my math instructor, his costume

Which made me laugh in reminiscences resumed.
Those days I left his classes because of his perfume.
Then I remembered the drama days in college.
They were very sweet, especially as I remembered vividly great actors.

THE EPILOGUE

I know what you are thinking about,
I will be fair to answer your doubts,
I am a genuine pro-feminist also by letter.
This I say for those who will read about me later.
Women deserve love; they are my epicenter.
I advocate their course as a present presenter.
I am happily married, husband and father.
Neither to Miss Angel nor to Miss Asunder.

They are all my fictional characters so noble,
Though not perfect, or at some point all fumble.
If you have not read any of my books,
Please, haste to get them with good looks.
Read about me in my books just as an author.
I don't write to breed racism, nor an agitator.
I was born a poet and playwright navigator
Not by scholastic nor any social innovator.

But I was born so, as created by my Creator.
I am of flesh, like you all trained by educators,
Many to whom I am indebted, not by debt,
But indebted by gratitude profound or in depth.
You have just read a bit of my biography,
Mostly real, and less amplified by philosophy.
Apart from this dramatic poetry written with velocity,
I am mortal with an immortal or eternal curiosity.

America must at all cost address today's atrocity,
Not with racial pride or brutish police viscosity,
But with its diplomacy, and even so, generosity.
Charity must begin at home in our very cities

Before we can be great again by philosophies.
Americans are troubled at heart for their porosity,
Covid-19, police kneeling on necks, animosity
Has wrecked every heart with sore ferocity.

Blacks are not whites' foes or enemies,
We are all brothers and sisters with envies.
There is only one law, love, not religiosity
We must live it, learn it fervently with prosody.
I know we are experts in criminal custody.
Let love rain, let it reign with all rhapsody.
The world has seen our frailties or monstrosity.
Now is time to play it wisely with much precocity.

Most often, it's all vanity upon vanity grandiosity
To gain the whole world but forfeit divine mercy.
Our conscience is the greatest form of tortuosity,
Not even our constitution in its present verbosity
Nor the media, always prone to report so gossipy.
We are like children in the market with loquacity,
Always entertained with stories of racial bellicosity.
Our history is tainted with blood or scrupulosity.

Our girls are entrapped with vanity and sinuosity,
And have departed from everything divinity or morality.
We pride in our laws, deprive others of affluence cozily.
If we are truly one nation, we need opportunity equality.
If we are truly one nation, we need one philosophy.
Everyone needs love, or deserves an apology
When their rights are denied with fake ideology,
When they are squashed like ants by mahogany.

Our existence or love is still an apostrophe,
We still need to earn this integrity or trophy
That will make us a nation under God's autonomy.
We as a nation are guilty of sins such as sodomy,
We all have free will to justify our dichotomy.
Someday, we will all stand to write our autobiography.
As we calculate every location traversed in geography

And every thought that rang in our hearts' philosophy.

That D-day,
You will tremble and forget your anthropology.
That D-day,
You will tremble and forget your archaeology.
That D-day,
You will tremble and forget your chromatography.
That D-day,
You will tremble and forget your endocrinology.
That D-day
 You will tremble and forget your iconography.
That D-day,
You will imagine what runs through minds.
That D-day,
You will also feel your own experiences
As on this D-day our hearts are hot to express ours.

GLOSSARY

Achu: A grassland dish in Cameroon eaten with soup on a banana leaf.

Ashawo. A Nigerian slang for prostitute.

DV: Diversity Visa.

Rue de la Joie: A place in Cameroon where prostitutes pose themselves for hire by men to satisfy their sexual desires.

Njangi: A form of monthly financial contributions. Each member of the group takes a huge sum of money contributed by others and also contributes for the next person.